THE MEDIOCRE LIFE OF

Jordan Gaites

ROBIN J. McKAY

authorHOUSE®

AuthorHouse™
1663 Liberty Drive
Bloomington, IN 47403
www.authorhouse.com
Phone: 1-800-839-8640

Published by AuthorHouse   2/27/2012

ISBN: 978-1-4685-3465-8 (sc)
ISBN: 978-1-4685-3467-2 (hc)
ISBN: 978-1-4685-3466-5 (e)

FORWARD

Like so many people, Jordan Gaites is happy with his life, but feels something is lacking. But unlike most people, Jordan has a secret past full of excitement that makes his present life seem drab. He is unable to share this past with his life-long friend Jack Lambert, and upon a reunion with Jack, Jordan is thrust into a conspiracy that involves murder and could have world-wide implication. Events unfold that bring to light some American history and legend that could significantly alter our current history books. Ultimately Jordan is faced with a dilemma on what secrets he should expose and what secrets would be best kept secret. But one thing is for sure. Jordan's life will never be mediocre again.

PROLOGUE

"I've got you beat this time Jack." Ten more feet and I will be at the top. We'd climbed this tree a dozen times over the last few weeks, but this would be the first time beating Jack to the top. It had become a regular stop on our way home from junior high. My left foot slipped on the next branch and I glanced down as I regained my footing and I could see Jack out of the corner of my eye. He was momentarily frozen and looking down. To the casual observer they might say he was scared to take the next step. But I knew better. Jack was intentionally holding back to let me beat him to the top. Once again I would pretend to not have noticed his intentional loss and I would gloat on my victory when we were both at the top. The alternative would be to embarrass Jack for his generosity and embarrass myself in acknowledging his charity and my inability to beat him yet again. I've no doubt that I've beaten Jack legitimately a few times during our perpetual competitions, but our good friendship was based partly on my attempts to prove to Jack that I was his equal and partly on his attempts to fool me into thinking it was true. We continued the competition in almost everything we did. Not so much to allow the charade to continue, but in a vain attempt to find skills that I really could challenge Jack on. I was pretty much Jack's intellectual superior, but a duel of computing math problems just doesn't give a 13 year old boy quite the same thrill as a tree climb or bike race. Maybe in our adulthood I would have the opportunity to impress Jack in something other than our childhood games. Friendships like ours were eternal.

CONTENTS

CHAPTER I

OLD FRIENDS

OUR FINEST CRYSTAL ADORNED THE dining room table fitted with the tablecloth my wife Marcy had purchased earlier today. This would only be the second occasion we've had to break out the fine china I got Marcy last year for Christmas. We weren't much for entertaining, and it just never seemed right to use the fine china for just a meal for the two of us. I slowly toured the house to see if there was anything else out of place for this evening's engagement. I've looked forward to this evening for over two weeks now. Jack Lambert, my closest and dearest high school buddy was coming over for dinner. He was attending a cosmetic surgery convention in Los Angeles for the weekend and thought it was an opportune time to catch up. Jack had always excelled in everything he did. What made Jack so special to me was the fact he never relished in his successes. On the other hand, I fired off rockets and flares on those rare occasions that I bested him in some trivial task like flicking bottle caps into a trash can or seeing who could drink a large glass of milk the quickest. Now I had the monumental task of convincing him that I had also been successful in life since our high school graduation 10 years earlier. Much has happened since Jack and I graduated from high school.

After high school Jack went on to graduate from Harvard with honors without even really having a firm plan for his career. Eventually he decided on cosmetic surgery and went on to get his doctorate to become one of the best cosmetic surgeons our country has ever seen. Jack had set up his practice in Chicago and wealthy patients from all over the world came to him for adjustments to their personal appearance. I stayed in touch with Jack via email and while I feigned ignorance on his achievements in our emails, I actually tracked his success with the same intense interest I tracked his achievements in our school days. It was somewhat of a relief that I was no longer in competition with him for popularity though. Even though I was happy for his success I still couldn't help but feel the jealousy that instilled the competition that highlighted our friendship in our youth.

I, on the other hand went into law enforcement right after high school. I had always enjoyed puzzles and brain teasers as a kid, and then became intensely interested in detective movies as I grew older. I always prided myself in being able to identify the guilty person by the clues before the show revealed who the culprit was. Becoming a detective was my dream, so I entered the Los Angeles police academy. I graduated with honors and was well on my way to a brilliant and exciting career in law enforcement. I spent three years walking a beat biding my time while studying for the detective exam. Eventually I got recommended to take the exam and I passed it the first time I took it. This was only the first hurdle to becoming a detective. Detective applications still had to be reviewed by a board and I patiently waited for another three weeks after passing the exam to hear the board results. When the good news came it meant that I would officially become the youngest member of the Los Angeles police force to make detective. But fate can play mean tricks on you. Becoming a detective evidently just wasn't in the cards for me. One unfortunate day six years ago would now change my life forever. It was Friday of my last week on the beat and I would move to my new desk the following Monday. My mind was pre-occupied with how big a change my new position would be when I responded to a silent alarm from the 9th street Wells Fargo bank. I arrived just in time to intercept four bank robbers as they were leaving the bank. A long fierce gun battle ensued. While I was able to keep them pinned down until back-up arrived, I took a shot to the hip and an innocent by-stander was shot and killed by one of the suspects. While unofficially I was considered a hero by my fellow officers, the precinct was forced to condemn my actions based on the death of an innocent bystander and the massive damage done to cars and surrounding businesses from gunfire. Seems the local news stations were comparing me to Dirty Harry leaving death and mayhem all over the city's streets. My wound wasn't bad and I was ready to go back to the precinct in under a week, but I was still given an additional week of administrative leave by my Captain while they completed their internal investigation of my actions. My Captain called me two days prior to my return to work to inform me I had been cleared of any misconduct. He informed me that no punitive actions would be leveled against me. When I returned to the precinct that following week expecting to move into my new detective's position I was called into the Captain's office. I assumed I was going to be briefed on my new assignment and possibly receive a hand shake over my success in breaking up the bank robbery. But instead I was told that I was no longer considered to be detective material. What was even more humiliating was that this was done in the presence of a complete stranger standing next to my Captain. The Captain explained to me that the public would rather I had let the robbers escape if it would have saved the life of that bystander caught in the cross-fire. The Mayor was also concerned with all the gunfire damage to the surrounding businesses which he attributed to my reckless heroism. It seems the Los Angeles police force was again in the media spot-light and politics dictated that the force make an example of me. After delivering this bad news the Captain then introduced me to Mr. Dove standing next to him and then promptly stood up and left his office closing the door behind him. I wondered what part Mr. Dove would play in the department's obligation to make an example out of me. But instead he explained to me that he was not associated with the Police Department and was instead a representative from the CIA. He went on to explain that they were impressed by my detective exam scores. He acknowledged that while the public might not be impressed with the way I handled the bank job, the CIA was more interested in the details of my written report. Mr. Dove said that it was evident from my report that my handling of the situation was more instinctive than procedural. He said I used several tactics not taught in police training to keep four bank robbers at bay for almost 15 minutes until back-up arrived. It seems that the section of the detective exam involving analytical skills was what I excelled in most, and that was the particular area the CIA screened potential applicants for. Mr. Dove also explained to me that while the incident was going to be a blemish on my police force career it had no bearing on the CIA's interest in me. He said that if I were to consider joining the CIA I had the potential to rise through the ranks rapidly considering my ability to think and react quickly in stressful situations. He explained to me that the CIA had been considering me as a potential recruit even prior to the bank shoot-out. Having grown quite dissatisfied with being on the beat, and now anticipating that my application for detective would never be accepted, I chose to accept Mr. Dove's proposal.

The first 18 months of my career in the CIA were quite interesting though not necessarily exciting. I went through six months of training and then a little over a year doing some fairly boring operative work which was mostly just footwork and surveillance. But the next three years after that were quite different. I worked for the CIA for a total of five years of which the last two involved what most people would call black-ops. I did many things during those last two years I am not proud of. But I rationalized that my actions were in the best interest of the security of the United States. During this short and incredibly exciting career in the CIA two events happened as I reached my four year point. The first was running into Marcy, my high-school sweetheart. We had lunch together to reminisce and I didn't foresee the almost instant rekindling of our romance. Our high-school romance fizzled when she moved out of state to go to college and after four months of corresponding by mail we agreed to see other people. I had assumed she never returned to Los Angeles after college and then had a chance encounter with her at an espresso stand. It seems she had dreams of becoming a psychologist but ran out of funds for her education and returned to Los Angeles where she had been waitressing ever since leaving college. She mentioned thinking of looking me up a couple of times, but decided that I was probably a very successful person who wouldn't be interested in a relationship with a struggling waitress. After only one date with Marcy I was convinced that she was what was missing in my life. But now I had a huge dilemma. A romantic involvement at that point in my career was strictly forbidden and considered a security risk. While I was pondering the predicament I was in with my renewed infatuation with Marcy, the second event I mentioned earlier came up. An assignment opportunity was presented to me by the agency. The agency picked their four top covert field agents to present this assignment to. It was strictly a voluntary assignment because the assignment only had two possible outcomes. Either the agent would be captured and most likely executed as a spy while the United States denied any knowledge of the agent's activities, or if the assignment was successful the agency would be forced to discharge the agent from the CIA to protect itself. The agency assured the four of us that if the assignment was successful the monetary compensation would more than make up for the fact that whoever took the assignment would no longer be able to work for the CIA. Plausible deniability was a key aspect to black-ops. If the details of the assignment were ever to become public knowledge the agency required the ability to deny responsibility for the agent's actions. The agency wanted to be able to show that they discharged those involved immediately when the event happened. The agency could successfully sell a 'rogue agent' story and protect themselves if the actions of the agent became public at a later date, but only if they could show the agent was discharged as soon as his actions became known to the agency. Waiting until the story became public knowledge to take action would be too late to try and sell the 'rogue agent' story. The plausible deniability story required that the agency produce a legitimate paper trail showing the agency. While the severity of the actions of the agent might be considered criminal by some, the CIA would cite 'in the interest of national security' as an excuse for not prosecuting the agent. The monetary compensation for the agent would be well-hidden in a myriad of paperwork. This was the out I was looking for that would allow me to pursue a relationship with Marcy again. The only down side would be that once again, if my assignment ever became public, I would be denounced in public and praised in private. Just like the bank job with the Los Angeles police force. I met up with Marcy before my assignment and shared with her that there was something very important that I needed to do that would not allow me to be in contact with her for almost two months. I stressed that I was extremely interested in progressing our renewed relationship and I was doing something for the United States Government that would allow me to devote my full attention to her when I finished the assignment. I also stressed that this would be a very lucrative venture though I doubt Marcy was that impressed by money. While Marcy was uncomfortable with my inability to share my work with her, she assured me she would be waiting for me when I returned. Needless to say, the assignment was extremely successful or I wouldn't be sharing this story with you. While the agency was sorry to see me go, they rewarded me greatly for my success on that last assignment. My monetary compensation was buried in what the record would show was a series of very successful stock investments. I spent three days going through debriefings and signing non-disclosure agreements upon my return from the assignment. Those three days seemed to drag on forever since the only thing on my mind at that time was hooking back up with Marcy. Once I was actually out the door my intense interest in the CIA was replaced by my intense interest in Marcy. I proposed to Marcy three weeks after returning from the Middle East and she accepted. While I did not share the specifics of my assignments with her I did share with Marcy some generalities about my work with the CIA and my reason for leaving. She also resisted the questions she did not want to know the answers to, such as if I was required to kill anyone during my assignments.

But eventually even Marcy could not provide everything I needed in life. I still longed for mystery and intrigue. But something a little less life-threatening than covert ops was my goal. I didn't need anything to generate a lot of income since the CIA pretty much assured I would never again be in need of finances. So I eventually decided to convert my law enforcement and CIA cloak and dagger skills into a small private detective agency. This was more so to relieve my boredom than for anything else. While watching TV murder mysteries and working on brain teasers in a book did appease my boredom, they did very little in the form of physical exercise. I had no desire to become a couch potato before I reached my 30th birthday. But in reality, the appeal of being a Private Detective was not quite what I had imagined. So far my assignments have been limited to spying on unfaithful spouses, digging up dirt on business associates and finding missing persons that really weren't missing but only wished to be left alone. While not the same excitement of either my beat on the police force or my covert CIA missions, it at least kept me active. I've always considered my life to be a success despite the public disgrace of the botched bank job shoot-out. A wonderful wife, a moderately sized house, brown Labrador retriever in the back yard; I'm living the dream. But unfortunately, compared to Jack my life now was the epitome of mediocrity. Life as a private detective is infinitely more mundane than made out on TV shows. I am sure Jack would be impressed with the details of my assignments in the CIA, but unfortunately I would be unable to share them with him. The irony was that even though I finally had experiences that would trump Jack's, I couldn't even share them with him.

Now Jack was coming over for dinner and while I did not anticipate the same competition we experienced in high school, most certainly he would gather some indication of my life successes from my home surroundings. I dusted off my police trophies and certificates and moved a few of them out to the living room's fireplace mantle for this auspicious occasion. I meticulously moved furniture and decorations trying to come up with an arrangement to make our humble dwelling look more appealing to what I thought would be Jack's fine taste. But no matter how much I rearranged I could not make our dwelling look any more prosperous than it was. While my CIA pension certainly allowed Marcy and I to have a much more luxurious life-style, it just wasn't us. We would always still eat out at fast-food restaurants and wear Levi jeans. The lavish life-style that Jack was used to as evident by the various magazine articles I had read up on suddenly made the life-style I was so proud of look drab in comparison.

But my proudest achievement? Marcy! I prominently displayed our wedding pictures by the hutch that Jack would see as he entered the front door. It was not necessarily an attempt to rub Jack's nose in the fact that I won the heart of a girl we both had eyes for in our school days, but more of a gesture to show Jack that I will never forget what an impact his friendship has been on my life. Jack played an important part in my life by introducing Marcy to me in junior high. Jack knew I was shy with the girls and set me up with Marcy for our 8ᵗʰ grade prom even though it was obvious he found her just as attractive and I did back then. But now, knowing that Jack was still single, there was also the subtle hope that this might be one aspect of my life that Jack might envy.

The doorbell! This was it. The moment of truth. Marcy eyeballed me sensing my tension and concern about making a good impression. She had given me her full support in the folly of rearranging our furniture. I must have given her the impression I was out to prove to Jack that my life was more than what both her and I had previously agreed was perfect prior to Jack's phone call two weeks earlier. Gracefully she accepted this without even a hint that our masquerade was any sign of my dissatisfaction with our life. I opened the door and suddenly my wife and I both felt overdressed. There was Jack in blue jeans and his Los Angeles Lakers' championship T-Shirt. My wife glanced down at the ground and I could tell she was holding back a giggle. Jack was at least 50 pounds heavier than he was at our High School graduation and his receding hair line was so prominent he appeared much older than I anticipated. I am quite sure this is what amused my wife so much. All my tensions were suddenly gone. Here was my childhood bud that was causing a virtual flood of emotions and memories of our younger days.

"Jordy, long time no see!" That is what Jack called me in our school days and I doubt he would ever call me anything else.

"Jack, it's so good to see you again." I responded.

We embraced and Jack gave Marcy a quick hug while she smirked at me over his shoulder.

"I'll go grab you two a couple of beers and let you get reacquainted." Marcy said as she excused herself.

"I've been on the wagon for close to three years now Marcy. Do you have anything non-alcoholic?" Jack replied

"Will some unsweetened Ice Tea or root beer work?" Marcy asked.

"Tea will be fine." Jack responded.

"Tea it is." Marcy responded.

As Marcy exited the room Jack stepped back from me and gazed at my attire.

"I hope you and Marcy didn't dress up just for me? I'm guessing you have been deceived by the media and have seen pictures of me in my 'media garb'."

"Media garb?" I asked.

"I have an image to maintain. It's an unfortunate fact that people wanting to improve their own appearance will judge the abilities of their surgeons based on his own appearance. They refuse to accept that I might be totally at ease with being a slightly obese, balding middle aged man. So for photo shoots I had a special girdle and toupee designed specifically for me. But tonight you are seeing the real me. I dropped off my media garb at the hotel before coming over here and will don it tomorrow for my seminar presentation."

"Seminar presentation?" I asked

"Tomorrow I will unveil a new plastic surgery technique that I and my colleagues have been working on for a few years. It has the potential of replacing all the current conventional cosmetic surgery methods we use today. You are quite welcome to come to my seminar where you will be able to see me adorned in all my regalia for my public appearance."

"I think Marcy and I will pass on that one Jack. Cosmetic surgery is really not our cup of tea."

"Speaking of cup of tea, here you go Jack." Marcy said as she reentered the room with Jack's tea and my beer.

The next few hours went very well. Jack was the same person I remembered. Inflating my second place position much more than it deserved was nostalgically typical. He spent a good portion of the first hour asking about my police and detective work commenting on how much more exciting it must be than his drab (but world famous) cosmetic surgeon business. After sharing a few of my somewhat exciting interactions with street thugs while on the police force Jack started inquiring about what I've been up to the last four years. I was able to share with him that I spent those years working for the CIA, but I was obligated to tell him it was just a desk job with no excitement whatsoever. This was part of my separation agreement I signed during that long security debriefing. Jack was already familiar with my reasons for leaving the police force through past emails we had exchanged, but he was unfamiliar with how much the discharge from the police force played a part in my CIA recruitment. So I explained to Jack that I thought my desk job's investigative abilities helped the CIA much more than they ever would have helped the Los Angeles police department as a detective hoping that would be sufficient to impress him without revealing more than I was allowed to. I also shared this in an attempt to belittle the negativity surrounded my departure from the Los Angeles police department. Fortunately the agreed upon cover story for my departure from the CIA held much more truth than the rest of what I shared with Jack. Separating from the CIA for family reasons was quite often a plausible reason used for such cases but in my case it was much more fact than fiction. Jack politely agreed that I must have been a great asset to the CIA and they must have been sorry to see me go. I could sense that even though Jack's physical prowess was one I was never able to match in youth he had always respected my intellectual prowess as being superior to his. But of course in youth the studs get the girls and the nerds get the chess club trophies. After a long time enduring Jack's over-dramatization of the various experiences I'd had with the police force I mustered up the courage to dive into questions about Jack's lucrative career. He downplayed it quite a bit, but as much as he pumped me for information on my drab life, I felt compelled to reciprocate with interest in his career.

"Come on now Jack. Certainly there are some interesting cases or clients you have encountered?"

I expected maybe one or two short patient stories but instead opened the door for a quite lengthy response from Jack. As I would come to find out later, Jack would be reluctant to share any details about his clients considering anonymity was one reason he was sought out by the financial elite.

"Well Jordy, come to think of it, I had a very unusual case just this morning before closing up shop for the week. Maybe you could exercise your investigative abilities on this mystery."

"How's that?" I responded

"I could have sworn it was the president himself coming to visit me. I had cleared the afternoon of appointments and was getting ready to close up the office for the week and head home to pack for this weekend when I received a knock on my office's back door. This door leads to an alley that I utilize for special clients that want to keep their cosmetic procedures strictly confidential or for patients with extreme disfigurations that would be reluctant to be seen on the public street adjacent to the front door. I opened the door to see a black stretch limousine and two men having all the appearance of secret service agents. But before I could even ask the men what I could do for them, they quickly opened the back door to their limousine and escorted the occupant into my back office. This occupant wore a full length hooded trench coat, so I assumed disfiguration was the reason this potential client chose to use the back door. Many of my clients prefer not to be seen in public or be scrutinized in the waiting room so I did not confront this individual in the alleyway, but instead chose to let the three of them in without question. After they had entered and I closed the back door behind them I figured it was time to discuss how I could be of assistance. The stranger then dropped his hood and I could see he was an elderly gentleman around mid-60s, grey hair and while he did not appear to have any severe disfigurations he did have numerous small scars covering his face and hands. I can only assume that these scars might also encompass other portions of his body covered by his clothing. He introduced himself as Jeremiah Sweinstein and immediately started quizzing me on my research into skin-melding therapy."

"Skin-melding therapy?" I inquired.

"That's the new procedure I mentioned earlier this evening that I will be presenting to the convention tomorrow. It's a technique that me and my other three associates have worked on over the years. It involves a chemical concoction that alters the elasticity of skin on a temporary basis allowing limited molding of skin in such a manner that it does not exhibit any of the long-lasting ill-effects of present day plastic surgery techniques while keeping nerve endings intact. The plastic looking faces that cause many of our childhood movie stars to become camera shy in their old age is the side effect this new technique would alleviate. In effect, skin-melding allows your skin to take on the traits of putty for a very short period of time and allows reshaping the skin and the associated blood vessels and nerve endings simultaneously. By applying oxygen to the skin in a precise amount during the hardening process I have come up with a method to recreate the pores needed to allow the newly shaped skin to breath freely and appear natural. There is a limit to how much manipulation can be done without damaging the circulatory system and nerve endings but the potential for rectification of small injuries and scars will be monumental. This technique is still in its early trial stages, and knowing the limitations of just how far you can manipulate the skin without any serious side effects is paramount to my being able to offer this procedure to the public. Up until this morning I had only tested the procedure on immobile patches of skin on six test patients. An even then it is only on very small unobtrusive patches of skin that are either covered by clothing or beneath hairlines. I am the only one of my associates performing the procedure on a trial basis and we have not yet shared any results with the public. All my patients have signed extensive waivers and I have financially compensated them greatly for their participation in this study. While I am seeing remarkable success in my trials I still have further tests before this procedure can be offered on an out-patient basis. I've been examining the six trial patients frequently and I'm almost satisfied that there are no long lasting ill-effects but I still need to understand the limits of how far I can manipulate the skin without any negative effects. My colleagues and I will be sharing our papers and research with the cosmetic surgeon world this weekend at the convention for the first time. So I am extremely confused as to how this total stranger knew about something that only I and my three colleagues know about."

"But if your clients wish to remain anonymous, why are you sharing his name with me Jack?

"Because I am convinced that is not his real name. I'm hoping I can count on you to be discreet if you are able to solve this mystery for me."

Jack returned to his story about the mysterious stranger's visit.

"I asked the gentleman what interest he had in my research. He matter-of-factly pointed at his facial scars. I told him that while I am not sure what he has heard about skin-melding, the procedure is only in testing phase and only being tested on single small non-visible scars on trial patients. I also shared that while I was optimistic about the procedure's use on facial scars the next phase of my testing would be on scars near frequently flexed skin such as elbows and knees. I explained to him that this phase must be complete prior to testing the feasibility of using the procedure on frequently flexed facial tissue such as that near the mouth and eyes. I told him that it was still going to be some time before I was willing to try my procedure on the general public. I make it very clear that I already had the test patients I needed but if he were to leave his name and contact information I could contact him when I have more definitive results concerning the procedure's availability to the general public. The gentleman said this was unacceptable and that he wanted to become one of my test subjects. He practically demanded that I perform the procedure on a few of his scars immediately to see if they could be repaired. I responded by telling him that while this procedure shows great potential for correction of his scar tissue, that his face is covered with so many little scars that even if I was able to test it on him, it would be on non-visible scars and would not visibly alter his present situation. He became extremely agitated at this point raising his voice to tell me he MUST know the potential of this new technique NOW! He then insisted I perform the procedure on him immediately. There was an unpleasant silence at that point where I glanced at the two body guards present to gauge whether I thought I was in any danger at this point."

"Jack, this sounds dangerous and you might be wise going to the police about this." I interrupted.

"Let me finish my story and you decide." Jack responded. "The stranger then reached inside his overcoat pocket and my heart missed a beat until he pulled his hand out and slapped a stack of $100 bills on the table. I could see that the paper ring around the wad indicated there was $10,000 in this stack. I expressed my concern about the ethical aspect of performing the procedure in this manner. I told him that if he would fill out the paperwork to become one of my test patients I could get him in within two weeks after I return from Los Angeles. He snapped back that this was unacceptable and then proceeded to slap down another $10,000 stack of bills. I told him this was highly unusual, but after another glance at the stoic faces of his escorts I conceded to perform the procedure on a couple of unobtrusive scars if he would fill out the required paperwork while I prepared the equipment and chemicals. Jordy, you must understand I did not do this for the money but to get myself out of a very uncomfortable situation. I was scared of what would happen if I had refused. I'm not sure if I was in any physical danger, but it was obvious that this man was not going to accept no for an answer."

"Who else have you told about this Jack? I still think this situation could be dangerous."

I haven't told anyone Jordy. I do not want to jeopardize my reputation for discretion if I'm just overreacting to an unusual situation. It's possible the stranger is just worried about his confidentiality. After conceding to test the procedure on him, I explained to him that I would only perform the procedure on a few of his small scars hidden beneath his hairline, and a few of his scars below collar level to minimize the impact should he not be happy with the results. He was satisfied with this concession which surprised me considering I would not be treating the most prominent scars on his face. But he also insisted that I treat an area on his neck that experienced repeated flexing. This was when I became convinced that he truly was more interested in the potential of the procedure than an immediate improvement to his current appearance. The tension of the situation seemed to settle at this point and I then went to my filing cabinet and pulled the required test subject paperwork out of my filing cabinet for my mysterious stranger. I returned to my treatment room and explained to him that I needed to draw a blood sample from him to adequately prepare the chemicals I would be using on his scars. He asked why a blood draw was needed and I explained that it was simply for blood-typing. The chemicals I prepare permeate the skin and trace amounts remain below the skin for a few weeks. The concoction must match his blood type to prevent his body from rejecting the chemicals and causing a severe skin reaction. Without the blood-typing, the potential exists to cause a scar more severe than that which the procedure is attempting to remove. For a moment I thought this blood draw was going to be a deal breaker and there was a deathly silence in the room as he pondered my request. Just as I thought he was going to about-face and leave he sat down and rolled up his sleeve and said he was ready to begin. As I prepared the chemicals and equipment in my lab I could hear whispers from the other room. It appeared that Mr. Sweinstein was concurring with his escorts on the manner in which the forms were to be filled out. Due to the collaborative effort I overheard I have serious doubts as to the accuracy of the information this gentleman provided me."

"So are you asking my assistance in finding the identify of this person?" I asked.

"Maybe if I know who it is I am dealing with I can get over my nervousness about this encounter. It's more about my feelings of guilt concerning the legitimacy of the transaction than actual physical danger I am concerned. Despite a very uncomfortable silence during the whole procedure, it went off without a hitch from that point on. Other than being $20,000 richer for the event and a little more rushed at getting to the airport for my flight to Los Angeles I saw no downside for this arrangement. His insistence on doing an area of repeated skin movement might very well expedite making my procedure available sooner. I'm trying to suppress my suspicions that I will never see this gentleman again. To appease my conscious about treating this gentleman I must be able to evaluate the success of his treatment. I suspect he might never return to me to show me the results."

"I would think, based upon the tension with his visit, that him not returning would be a good thing." I suggested.

"Not for my conscious." Jack replied. "I rationalized jumping a step in my testing based on being able to evaluate how successful his treatment would be on that one area of his neck. If I never see him again then my skipping a step in my testing will have solely been for monetary gain. I'm not comfortable with that."

I thought about what Jack was saying for a minute, then responded. "But what if I uncover that this gentleman is a dangerous person? He might not take kindly to you knowing his true identity."

"That is why I am sharing this with you Jordy. If you find out who this is, and decide he is a dangerous person, I will not pursue it any further. I will be able to pacify my guilt for accepting his money without any benefit to my research. Considering the number of untreated scars he still has I believe he will eventually want more of this treatment. If he is truly dangerous, then hopefully he will visit another surgeon for this procedure after it becomes available publicly. Maybe he was just very impatient to know what the future might hold for his condition."

"But this is your procedure, wouldn't he have to return to you?" I asked.

"Not necessarily. I will own the rights to the technique, but hopefully this procedure will eventually be available everywhere. I am both anxious and apprehensive about a potential follow-up visit. I helped rationalize my discomfort in the manner in which this testing was done by jotting down the license plate of their vehicle as they drove away. While I may have bent my own ethical standards a bit in accepting the $20,000 cash, I rationalized that Mr. Sweinstein and his thugs were not going to accept no for an answer and I had no choice. By my writing down their license plate number I have eased my conscious a bit in the hopes of solving this mystery. Even if I never intended to act upon that information, the piece of paper I placed in my pocket still helped calm my nerves. After they left I sat down at my computer and googled the name Jeremiah Sweinstein. As I suspected I couldn't find anyone with that name in the greater Chicago area. I still have the license plate number here in my shirt pocket and probably would have just thrown it out later. But since you mention your frustration in having any challenging cases, maybe you would like to look into this one for me? You are probably the only person I would trust with this Jordy. I believe you could maintain the discretion I so desperately need for this situation."

"I will see what I can do for you Jack. Tracing a license plate would hardly be interpreted as an investigative challenge, but maybe I can use it to find the information you need. I still have some friends at the police department that can help me with this."

"I don't want the police involved."

"Don't worry Jack. I have a friend or two that can trace a license plate number with no questions asked. As for finding other information on your mysterious stranger? I can't make any promises, but leave the license plate number with me and I will see what I can do for you."

After an excellent dinner served by my wife (she went overboard for me on this one), we again retired to the den for another hour of reminiscing about our school days. Being so exceptionally pleased with my marriage to Marcy and my gratitude to Jack for that fateful day in 8th grade where Jack introduced us, I asked Jack a question.

"So Jack, is there a special someone in your life we don't know about?" I asked. Maybe this was another attempt on my part to prove to Jack that I was more fortunate than him without being as famous as him.

"I don't have a whole lot of free time to play the dating game. I do however have my eye out for a particularly charming countess I met during my last visit to Italy. I will most likely look her up during my next visit in a few weeks."

"Was she one of your clients?" I asked.

Jack frantically shock his head no.

"I make it a point to never have a personal relationship with a client. In my business that would be career suicide. I met her at a fashion show that one of my clients was in. We seem to have hit it off pretty well. I believe she is as intrigued by me and I am her. I'll know better during my next visit to Florence."

Jack didn't elaborate much more and I decided not to pry any further. After a little more idle chitchat Jack mentioned that it was getting a little late and that he had numerous events to attend in the morning. I suggested we get together one more time before his return to Chicago and he agreed. Jack suggested he would look over the weekend's itinerary first and get back to me on when would be a good time to hook up. Marcy and I escorted Jack to the door commenting on how pleasant the evening had been seeing him again after all these years. I bid Jack farewell and off he went to his hotel and weekend convention of cosmetic surgeons.

I felt extremely comfortable with myself and my life the rest of the evening after Jack's departure. Due to always feeling threatened by Jack's success I had never revealed to Marcy that Jack had also wanted to take her out that first time we both saw her back in Junior High. But Jack was able to get almost any girl he wanted and he chose to introduce Marcy to me instead when I shared with him that I also was attracted to Marcy. But after this evening and seeing Jack's appearance I was feeling pretty secure in my marriage and figured that Marcy would no longer find Jack as appealing as he was in our high school days. Marcy and I snuggled by the fireplace for a hour and watched TV that evening before going to bed and I shared with her some of the more personal things that Jack and I had shared during our school days, including the discussion we had about her when we both first saw her.

"That's sweet to know Jordy, except that you were the one who first caught my eye and not Jack. Jack seemed a little too popular for me, and I wanted a boyfriend that was a little tamer I guess." Marcy reassured me.

"Tamer? Is that what I was to you?" I said with a hint of disappointment. She only gave me a sheepish smile and snuggled closer. I suggested that we drive up the coast the next morning or just spend some time on the beach the next day and enjoy the weekend. We got up fairly early the next morning and drove all the way to Santa Barbara. We ate at one of our favorite Mexican restaurants and then stopped at a few vegetable stands along Highway 1 coming back home early in the afternoon. My wife commented on how Jack was still the same lovable guy he was in high school despite his dramatic change in appearance. She also was puzzled at why someone with such a talent for improving the appearance of others would do nothing about his own receding hairline and slight obesity. I responded that it was just Jack, always confident, never self-conscious. I suggested that maybe we could call Jack when we got home and see if he had found a slot in his itinerary to hook up with us again before returning to Chicago. Marcy agreed, and upon arriving back home I immediately went to the phone and dialed up Jack's hotel. I asked for Jack's room and the operator put me on hold for quite some time. Finally a different person got online and informed me that Jack was not in his room. I asked if I could leave a message and there was another long pause. Then the person on the other end of the phone informed me that Jack had checked out and was no longer a guest at the hotel. This confused me greatly since I knew Jack had the same hotel booked for the weekend so I asked when he checked out. The person simply responded that they were not at liberty to discuss such matters over the phone at this time. I was not aware hotel privacy rules extended to this information, but I decided to not inquire further and decided to find Jack's cell phone number which I had written down on a notepad in the living room. I returned to the living room to inform Marcy that Jack had checked out of his hotel and found her standing in the middle of the room, TV remote in hand, with her mouth wide open. I asked her what was wrong but before I could get an answer, my gaze shifted to the television where there I saw Jack's picture pasted on the screen. I quickly grabbed the remote and turned up the volume but it was already apparent through the scrolling text at the bottom of the screen that world renowned plastic surgeon Jack Lambert had fallen to his death from his hotel balcony only two hours earlier. My wife and I both stood there dumbfounded trying to grasp the full story, but they only had bits and pieces about a world-renowned cosmetic surgeon falling to his death. They eventually elaborated that there was no evidence of foul play and that the police were investigating the possibility of it being an accident. Then the news reported that there was an unsubstantiated report that someone might have seen him jump.

Chapter 2

The Circumstances Surrounding Jack's Death

I IMMEDIATELY CALLED THE POLICE department to inquiry about the events surrounding Jack's death. Unfortunately my first inquiries into Jack's death met the typical precinct canned responses. But after a little professional private investigative work I was able to find out more. Okay, actually I just waited a bit and then called back and asked if Peter Kirby was still stationed at the precinct. Pete was my old beat partner who had called in sick that fateful day four years ago when I had the bank shoot-out. The front desk operator informed me that Detective Kirby was at his desk and transferred me. "Detective" Kirby! That made me smile and I had to wonder if my separation from the force had expediting his advancement. I also wondered how different my life would have been if it had been myself that had called in sick that day instead of Pete. When Pete came on the line he immediately recognized my voice and thought it was a social call until I explained to him my friendship with Jack Kirby and the reason for my call.

"Jordy, I really don't understand what you want from me. I understand Jack was a close friend of yours, but I'm only an investigating officer in the case and not the detective in charge. I don't really have any information that I can share with you."

"What's this rubbish about someone seeing Jack jump? I just had dinner with Jack last night and he was **not** suicidal Pete!"

"Don't shoot the messenger Jordy. As far as I know, the statement about the possibility of suicide is a statement any precinct would put out given the circumstances."

"What circumstances would those be Pete?"

"You know I can't discuss that with you. This is an open investigation."

I was becoming frustrated with the obvious stonewalling I was getting from someone I had once considered to be a close ally in the fight against crime.

"The television is giving me more information that you are Pete. They are saying someone claims they saw him jump. What if I had information pertinent to this investigation? Would you then discuss it with me?"

"You're asking me to go way out on a limb here Jordan. I am required to advise you to take any information you might have to the detective in charge."

"I don't know the detective in charge Pete, I know you! You can tell them I refused to give this information to anyone other than you. Maybe this can even earn you a few brownie points on this case."

"What information do you have Jordy? I'm under the impression there is no evidence of foul play in this and all the current evidence is supporting either a suicide or accidental death."

"Jack had a client yesterday morning that went through great pains to cover his identity and Jack gave me his license plate number to look up for him because of the suspicious behavior involved." I informed Pete.

"Jack saw a client here in Los Angeles yesterday?" Pete asked.

"No, it was back in Chicago before he caught his flight to Los Angeles." I responded.

"Certainly you have more than that Jordy? Isn't it a known fact that many people don't wish that their cosmetic enhancements become public? I would imagine that many of Jack's clients would prefer their procedures be kept secret."

"From the public? Yes! But this gentleman concealed his identity from Jack who is world-renowned for his discretion with his clients. This procedure was not an enhancement but a treatment for a facial scar that obviously was already visible to anyone who has already met this gentleman. There's more to this than simple discretion Pete. Something is not on the up and up with this client. He went through a great deal of effort and money to cover up his visit to Jack for a procedure that no one should be embarrassed about. Jack said he was concerned he might be in danger from the two suits accompanying the gentlemen and that he felt extreme pressure to perform this procedure that is only in trial phase. This is not a simple case of removing a facial mole on a distinguished client. Don't you find this unusual and slightly less than coincidental Pete? Jack was in high spirits last night. He was presenting this monumental new procedure to the cosmetic world this weekend. The very same procedure this cloak and dagger gentlemen demanded. Jack had everything to live for and was obviously excited about this weekend's convention."

"Jordy, I will share this with you for your own best interest but this in information we have not released. Your friend Jack called the suicide hotline minutes before his death. There is a half empty bottle of cheap wine spilled on the balcony, and it appears that even if Jack was having second thoughts about committing suicide, the possibility exists he slipped on the balcony and fell to his death accidentally. The front desk attendant stated that someone ran in from the street yelling that someone had jumped off of their balcony. When we arrived his door was locked from the inside with one of those latches that can only be done from the inside. We had to break that latch to access his room. We cannot rule out suicide based on the phone call, and we can't rule out an accident based on the puddle of wine and overturned chair on the balcony. But we can, I repeat can, but not necessarily have, rule out foul play if we don't come across any evidence supporting the contrary."

"I've got problems with that Pete. Jack doesn't drink, and even if he did drink, he wouldn't buy cheap wine. What did he say to the hotline? Jack didn't appear to be depressed in the slightest during dinner last night."

"Individuals considering suicide might do anything to dull the emotions and pain Jordan, you know that. The quality of his drink was probably not a concern. As far as his conversation with the hotline, from what I've been told he hung up on the hotline before they could get him to speak. This is quite typical of a person contemplating suicide but having second thoughts."

"Then anyone could have made that call before throwing Jack over the railing Pete. Certainly a phone call with no conversation isn't conclusive."

There was a long pause at this time. Pete was not answering my question and I was becoming agitated.

Pete responded in a very soft voice. "I could get in a lot of trouble for sharing this with you Jordy. You can't share this with anyone. I could lose my job here if anyone knew I was sharing this with you. There was another phone call made by Jack prior to the suicide hotline. It was to one of his clients. We questioned that client and it appears that Jack had been making repeated attempts to start a relationship with her. Your friend Jack was very distraught over her rejections."

"I don't buy it Pete. Jack and I discussed his love life last night and he shared with me that his only romantic interest is with a countess in Italy. He also informed me that he would never have a relationship with a client. Who is this client who claims Jack was making advancements towards her?"

"I can't share that information with you Jordy."

"Jack would never jeopardize his career trying to enter a relationship with a client. It's just unethical, and he wouldn't do it. This girl must be in on it Pete."

There was some more uncomfortable silence and I knew that Pete was considering me to be hysterically grasping at any straws to support a conspiracy to kill Jack. Pete finally responded.

"We verified the call was placed from Jack's cell phone to this client shortly before his death and we've already questioned the client. She expressed concern for losing her career if word got out that she received breast enlargement surgery from Jack's clinic. Jack's discretion with his clients is the reason people come to him Jordy, and the department needs to respect that confidentiality. Her cooperation with this investigation was based upon our keeping her identity private if at all possible. At this point there is no reason to doubt anything she has shared with us and we plan to honor her confidentiality request if at all possible. The two phone calls combined with the condition of the scene leads us to believe Jack may have committed suicide because of her rejection of his advances. You yourself stated that it would be unethical to court a client. Jack might not have been inclined to tell you about any inappropriate infatuation he might have had with her. Even if the suicide theory is incorrect, accidentally death could also be consistent with what we have examined at the scene. Jordy, I will do everything within my power to try and protect Jack's name, but we have to go where the investigation leads, and right now we are leaning towards suicide. We have no hard evidence of foul play for now."

"Can you at least look into this license plate number and see where that leads Pete?"

"I don't really see much potential for this license plate being a credible lead Jordan but I will stick my neck out for you on this and see if anything pops up. But unless the owner has some sort of criminal background or a link to Jack's death pops up I won't be able to pursue it any further. We must have some reason to question a client in Chicago concerning Jack's death in Los Angeles. There must be some link between the two before we can start questioning confidential clients. From what you described, this sounds like a prominent client that will not take kindly to being questioned by the police. You know the hot water we could get in here if we run into this guns ablazing."

"Well humor me and at least look into it. I will see if I can dig anything up to give you more reason to pursue this."

"Jordy, you are still admired greatly by everyone down here at the precinct and they think you got a bum deal with that bank job shoot-out, but I would advise you to not go vigilante on me here. Please leave the police work to the police department."

"You do your job Pete, and I'll do mine. I'll stay out of your way." Frustrated, I hung up the phone.

I planned on visiting the Sheraton to investigate Jack's death but needed to stage some props for my visit. By the time I could fabricate a few business cards and a couple other things I needed for the visit it was late afternoon, so I decided to visit the hotel the next morning in hopes of talking to staff that were on duty at the time of Jack's death.

The next morning I drove to the Sheraton to try and get information about the previous day's events. I started with the bellhops. I figured if I was going to get thrown out for asking too many questions, I should probably start with the little people who didn't possess the power to throw me out. Obviously the Sheraton would not consider a death in their hotel as anything other than undesirable negative press and would prefer the whole incident be over as quick as possible. I entered the hotel inconspicuously enough and plopped myself down in the plush lobby couch to observe what mood the staff was in. For 10 minutes I observed nothing out of the ordinary. Seemed like their normal daily hotel routine. I slowly became irritated that my old friend Jack had died here yesterday and everyone just continues on as if nothing happened. Finally a bellhop wandered close enough for me to ask him over without grabbing the attention of the desk clerk.

"Hey you, wanna earn a quick $100?" I asked.

"I don't have to do anything illegal do I?" he responded.

"I'm a journalistic reporter and I just need a little information on the death that took place here yesterday."

"I'm sorry, but my boss has already advised all the employees that we could lose our jobs if we share any information with reporters. This accident could damage the hotel's reputation."

"Why is that? Do you possess information that could damage the hotel's reputation?"

"Well, no. But I really need this job and as much as I would like that $100 I don't wish to lose my job."

"Tell you what. I don't want you to lose your job either, but I will still give you the $100 if you just answer one or two questions you are comfortable with. If you don't like the question, don't answer it. Easy $100. What do you say?"

"So, if I don't like any of your questions do I still get the $100?"

"That's the deal."

"Okay. I have a break in 15 minutes. Can you meet me around the corner at the donut shop?" he asked.

"I'll be there with a coffee and donut ready for you." I responded.

Well, that turned out to not be quite the worst deal I've made in my life, but hardly worth $100. Seems the bellhop wasn't even on duty when the accident happened. He confirmed that Jack was on the 23rd floor but declined to tell me what room. Other than that, he was a total moron who knew virtually nothing that I nor anyone else didn't see on the news. I still wasn't quite ready to approach anyone of importance with my questions that might get me thrown out so I slipped up the stairs to the 2nd floor and then caught the elevator to the 24th floor. I again took the stairs to go down one flight to the 23rd floor. It's a whole lot easier to be inconspicuous through a crack in a door than it is to be surprised when an elevator door opens to someone you'd rather not see you. I wasn't really sure if any of this stealthy movement was necessary or if I was just reverting to my CIA habits to ensure I wasn't being tailed. Room 2308 was near the north fire exit and still had the police crime scene tape covering the door. Not anticipating I would find a smoking gun inside the room I decided against jimmying the lock at a crime scene. At this point I had no plan. I was just wandering aimlessly hoping that something out of the ordinary would jump out and grab me. I did however notice surveillance video cameras at the ends of each hallway and also inside the elevator. So whoever played a hand in Jack's death should be recorded somewhere.

After some fruitless wandering around the inside and outside of the hotel I decided it was time to push my luck and I returned to the lobby to talk to the hotel manager. I presented myself to the desk clerk as being an insurance investigator hired by Jack's corporation to gather facts about

Jack's death and asked to speak to the hotel manager. When the manager arrived and asked how he could be of assistance I presented my ruse.

"Hello, I'm Paul Ralston from Liberty Mutual." I said as I handed him one of my recently created business cards. "I'm here on behalf of Jack Lambert's associates. They are concerned about preventing a scandal due to the news reports of suicide. I believe a scandal would not be in either the hotel's or their best interests. I was hoping you had a minute or two to discuss the situation."

There was a slight hesitation on his part, but then he responded.

"I really don't see where anything concerning this could shed a negative light on the hotel. I can only share with you what you have probably already seen on the news reports." He elaborated.

"The police and news reports suggest the possibility of suicide. I understand that someone has allegedly seen him jump. Would that person have also been a guest at your hotel?" I asked.

"On no, that was just a pedestrian on the street." He responded.

"So the pedestrian was questioned by the police concerning this?" I asked.

"Maybe you should talk with the police first, Paul." He said glancing again at my business card. "If you had talked with them first they would have told you that they got that information from our desk clerk. The pedestrian just ran into the lobby and yelled that someone had jumped and didn't hang around." He said with a little more suspicion on his face.

Hopefully the manager didn't see me wince at the word 'jumped'.

"Are you sure he used the word jumped and not fell." I asked.

"The clerk was pretty confident in his statement to the police." the manager responded. I heard a slight tone of satisfaction in his voice since it would be a lot harder to find a hotel liable for someone jumping than it would be for someone falling.

"We gave a description of the pedestrian to the police but nobody got his name."

This sounded a little too convenient to me. I think if I saw someone jump to his death I would share that information with the police and not just mention it to the front desk.

"Your hotel security cameras would contain a record of that along with anyone entering or exiting Jack's room shortly before his death, wouldn't they? I asked.

"Our video surveillance of the lobby and elevators have already been turned over to the police. The hallway video is continuously monitored by our security staff and not recorded. That would require a much more expensive and elaborate recording system to record all of our hallways. This is a very large hotel Mr. Ralston." He shared.

"So you just record the front lobby and elevator cameras." I said while scrawling notes on my notepad. "Was there any room service, messages or phone calls made to or from Jack's room in the hours leading up to the death?" I asked

"No activity at all preceding his jump. Why do you need this information? I have already given this information to the police and I believe that is where you should be getting it." The manager exclaimed with a now apparent apprehension he didn't have when answering my first question.

"You have to understand that Mr. Lambert had many investors involved in his corporation that have lost a significant asset. While Jack's investors have a huge loss here, there are other competitors that would benefit greatly from Jack's death. I am just trying to rule out the possibility of any foul play or actions on the part of others contributing to Mr. Lambert's death."

At this point I could see that the manager's wheels churning. I had chosen my words poorly and it was apparent that he took my statement about 'actions on the parts of others' to also include hotel staff.

"Sir, I can assure you there was nothing the hotel did to contribute to your client's death but I think any further questions you have about this should probably be addressed to the hotel's attorney. I'm afraid I must ask you to leave now." He spouted.

At about the time I figured out my tactical error here and that the manager was not going to respond to any further questioning by me, I caught the conversation going on to the left of me between two men in suits and the desk clerk. They were also discussing room service and phone records for room 2308. Out of the corner of my eye I could see they were showing the clerk their detective's badges. This looked like a very good time for me to depart since it was already apparent I had reached the limits of any information I would be able to get from the hotel staff. I really wanted to inspect Jack's hotel room but I felt that the risk of getting caught by investigators was too great. I thanked the manager for his time and informed him I had all the information I needed for now and that if I needed anything additional I would contact the hotel's attorney.

I was frustrated at not finding anything I would consider to be useful in proving Jack was murdered. I believed the only real chance of finding a good lead here at the hotel was inside Jack's room, but that just wasn't within my reach. If I hoped to continue my investigation without getting shut down by Pete and the precinct I would have to put that off until later. So far Pete was the only one knowing of my interest in Jack's death and if I hoped to keep it that way I needed to tread lightly in my investigation. I returned home and decided it was time to check on my only potential lead in this case; Jack's mysterious client. My wife was obviously concerned about my state of mind over Jack's death, so she sat by and watched and listened as I made my phone call to Peter Kirby. I had to call the precinct operator again but this time asked for Peter's phone extension so that I could call him directly next time without operator assistance. Pete answered after two rings.

"Pete. It's me, Jordan. Did you find anything out about the license plate number I gave you yesterday?"

"It's a dead end Jordan. It belongs to one of the corporate limousines for the DeLoreon Foundation. They won't give me information as to who was using the limousine two days ago without a warrant. I have nothing negative on the foundation that could justify me looking into who would have driven it to Jack's office in Chicago, and nothing linking the DeLoreon Foundation to Jack's death in a Sheraton hotel in Los Angeles. I'm sorry Jordan, but there's nothing else I can do for you."

"I'm sorry also. What about the hotel surveillance videos, did you find anything unusual on those?" I asked.

"Have you been putting your nose where it shouldn't be Jordy? We did in fact pick up those videos. Please let us do our job Jordy. I can't give you any specifics, but I will let you know if there are any breaks in the case that might change the scope of our investigation."

"You and I both know a hotel of that size has video surveillance, and it would be standard procedure for you to review those videos. I am only asking questions concerning standard procedure that I am quite familiar with Pete and not poking my nose where it shouldn't be." I defended myself.

"If I find out you're interfering with our investigation I will have to share it with my superiors Jordy."

"I'm not interfering Pete. Jack and I are life-long friends and I was hoping I still have a few friends down at the precinct also that would take this into consideration."

"Actually Jordan, the level of attention I am giving to the video tapes is not necessarily standard procedure considering the absence of any indication of foul play. I anticipated you not letting this go so I obtained the tapes myself this morning. I watched the entire hour preceding the death on both the lobby and elevator videos and saw nothing unusual. You need to let this go Jordan. Nothing good can come from this obsession of yours. If there is anything unusual about this we will find it and I will give you a call."

"Thank you for your help on this Pete. I won't forget it."

As I hung up Marcy grabbed and squeezed my hand and asked me if Pete had said anything useful. I shook my head to indicate he had not and then let her hand go and headed to my desk to access my computer.

A google of the DeLoreon Foundation gave me confidence that I did indeed have the correct license plate number for a couple of reasons.

The DeLoreon Foundation was a charitable foundation established in 1923 by John P. DeLoreon. The Foundation's beneficiaries included numerous worthy causes. Most of the beneficiaries they funded were on the top of the list of many other charitable foundations: Children's hospitals, Prosthetic limbs research, cerebral palsy, etc. However, when I did a little further research into what charitable causes had benefited most from the DeLoreon Foundation I came across sizable contributions into skin cancer treatment, skin grafting, and on top of the list: Cosmetic Surgery Research. Bingo! There has to be a connection here.

I did a little more research into the source of John DeLoreon's wealth used to fund his charitable foundation. It appears there was no single pot of gold at the end of the rainbow that made him wealthy. Over the years he acquired his wealth from numerous investments but the vast majority of his wealth was acquired from royalties on patents and inventions. It seemed that DeLoreon's researchers had also discovered numerous pharmaceutical medicines and devices only to sell either the production rights or ownership to other companies for a sizable profit. John DeLoreon seemed to have a knack for coming up with something good then abandoning it for a quick profit and moving on to something else if it didn't prove to be a long term income source. I could find very little information on John himself. It appears his wealth was inherited by his son Joseph sometime in the 1950's though I could not put an exact date to John's death. While the majority of the DeLoreon's assets were liquid, Joseph maintained ownership of Fracious, one of Europe's top cosmetic's lines and he was also the sole owner of a couple of resort hotels in the Bahamas. I could not find any specific information that could lead me to believe the mysterious visitor from the DeLoreon Foundation had anything to do with Jack's death, but I still had many unanswered questions:

Why would Jack mention to me a countess in Italy and not mention an infatuation with a young model in the United States? I firmly believed the model story was part of a cover-up for his murder.

Why would anyone give false information to a doctor with such a good reputation for discretion? Who was this man wanting to test Jack's new procedure? Whoever this was who visited Jack must have had a serious reason for keeping his identity secret other than just because of some cosmetic work. Was keeping that identity secret a motive for killing Jack, or was Jack's new procedure a potential new gold mine for the DeLoreon Foundation?

Joseph DeLoreon earned his fortune from patents and royalties. Could he have murdered Jack to steal his new procedure which no doubt would earn its owner a small fortune?

I refused to believe Jack would kill himself. Even if the investigators did eventually come to the conclusion that Jack slipped on the balcony and fell to his death, I was unable to believe the information about his phone call to the suicide hotline, or this young model that Jack supposedly became infatuated with.

My wife saw my disappointed expression at the end of my phone call to Pete and retired to the kitchen to prepare me yet another one of her special dinners. She reserves these special dinners for special occasions like Jack's visit or just those occasions when I am down in the dumps. Being down in the dumps had become a more frequent occurrence since leaving the exciting career I held in the CIA. Marcy returned from the kitchen and sat down beside me not knowing the information I had just Googled about the DeLoreon Foundation.

"So are you gonna drop this now and get on with your life Jordy? I'm so very sorry about Jack's death also, but life must go on for the rest of us. I've prepared one of your favorite dinners." she consoled me, while rubbing my shoulders.

"One last thing, and if I turn up nothing I'll put this behind me." I responded.

"What's that honey?' she asked.

"I need to examine Jack's office in Chicago."

Chapter 3

The Windy City

After dinner I retired to my study and began preparations for going to Chicago. I was able to determine that three airlines had interconnecting flights to Chicago the next morning but none of them had any vacancies. I put myself on standby for all three airlines and planned to hang out at the airport the next morning until something came up. So for the remainder of the evening I pulled out my bag of tricks and started preparing for the trip. My "bag of tricks" contains the normal variety of props that Private Detectives use for this type of investigative work along with a few not-so-normal items I had acquired from my cloak and dagger days. I stayed up late that night finding out everything I could about Jack's practice in Chicago and staged my bag of gadgets to get myself into the front door.

The next morning I didn't have any luck getting out on the first flight in the morning but there was a delay in the arrival of an international flight that opened up several seats on their connecting flight to Chicago. I brought with me all the information I could gather about Jack's clinic and practice to assist me in my plan to access his office and files. It appears that even though Jack was the sole practitioner at his office his three associates that shared some clients based on their particular area of expertise. These associates had their own private practices at other locations including one located back in Los Angeles near where I lived. These associates were also involved in Jack's skin-melding research and my investigation would most likely lead to them eventually, but I wanted to see what I could find in Jack's office first. I rented a car from Hertz at the Chicago airport but before I left the airport I took advantage of their free WiFi to look at a Chicago map and find a hotel with internet access right around the corner from Jack's office. Turns out it was a flea-bag hotel that typically rented rooms by the hour, but it would serve my purpose. I took an hour to settle in and unpack my props and dress accordingly for my presentation ahead.

Private detective information gathering abilities have been greatly enhanced by the latest technological advances. Color laser printers and cheap lamination machines now allowed most anyone to create identifications for most any purpose. The key to any successful private investigator is hinged on his ability to elicit information people might not want to share with your typical stranger. Thus said, I had several new business cards prepared for the trip. I chose to use the insurance investigator role again for my planned access to Jack's files. But I felt I needed an insurance company with a little more prestige than Liberty Mutual to elicit the cooperation I would need. I quickly donned my insurance investigator garb, or at least to the best of my knowledge what I would expect an insurance investigator to wear. My briefcase was an integral part of many of my roles, and I happened upon a store that designed and manufactured plastic logos you could affix to a briefcase or other device for various situations. For this situation I affixed an "L of L" logo to the front of the briefcase. It's amazing what a small cheap prop can do towards supporting a masquerade. The front door to Jack's office was unlocked so I entered and promptly introduced myself to the receptionist.

"Hello, I'm David Miles from Lloyds of London, are you Jack Lambert's receptionist?" I asked as I again handed my business card. Immediately handing a business card is a convenient distraction from any possible mistakes in a disguise. The receptionist gazed at the business card for about 5 seconds and then looked back up at me.

"My name is Stella. How may I help you?" she responded.

After blowing my poorly worded presentation with the hotel manager, I had rehearse in my head many times how I planned to entice the cooperation of Jack's receptionist.

"Stella, I am here on behalf of Jack and his associates. Jack's death is a detrimental blow to not only his own practice, but also to his associates. Jack's associates are the beneficiaries of an insurance policy covering the partnership. The amount of the payout will be based not only on a set amount for Jack's death, but also on lost income from his practice here in Chicago until he can be replaced. This lost income figure can only be ascertained by evaluating Jack's fees, client base and currently scheduled appointments."

I flashed some paperwork I had prepared and then immediately started feeding her more information to distract her from scrutinizing my fake information.

"I already have here Jack's figures for the past few years, but Jack's insurance policy will also take into account the potential income from his clients based on his upcoming schedule."

I could see apprehension in Stella's eyes as to her still not knowing exactly what it was that I wanted from her, and not knowing if she had the authority to give me what I would be asking for. I could also see stress in Stella's composure not knowing if she was out of a job or who would issue her next paycheck for work already completed, so hopefully she keyed into my comment about a replacement for Jack. I spewed out some more information about the impact Jack's death would have on his practice bringing Stella almost to the point of tears. I gauged her for a second and then decided it was time to reel her in.

"Stella, I am also going to need your time cards for the last few weeks so we can determine how much your next paycheck will be and I would like to know if you would be willing to continue to man the office until Jack's associates can get a replacement surgeon in to take over the practice? Would you be willing to continue as the receptionist here when a replacement can be acquired?" I asked.

I could see the stress and apprehension melting away as Stella was now contemplating the possibility of not being out of a job.

After a long hesitation she replied

"Why yes Mr. Miles. I would definitely be willing to stick around." She was able to stutter in relief.

I felt bad about misleading Stella and getting her hopes up, but this ploy was the edge I needed to get Stella to drop her guard and no longer look at me as a stranger. The end result of whatever became of Stella's position here was inevitable regardless of the line I was feeding her. I made a mental note to see what I could do to help her out when my investigation was all said and done because despite my cut-throat days in the CIA I still had a soft heart and felt bad about giving Stella false hopes at this point.

"Ok Stella, first things first. Jack's appointments for today. Did you already call and cancel those appointments? If so, call them back and let them know we will be in touch with them in the next week or so to reschedule their procedures with Jack's replacement. We would hate to lose them as clients. Anyone calling to schedule new appointments will need to call back next week once we have a better feel for how long Jack's office will be closed. I will need to ascertain the profit loss for at least this week and an estimate for the loss for each additional week until the replacement can arrive, and for that I will need access to Jack's client files."

I could see she was uncomfortable with giving me access to Jack's files, but it was no longer because of her apprehension of me as a stranger, but more so because of strict rules enforced by Jack himself. She informed me that Jack had strict rules that no one access those files except her and Jack unless he specifically gave her instructions otherwise.

"Well Stella, I understand the need for Jack's client's confidentiality, but getting permission from Jack at this point is pretty much out of the question. Wouldn't you agree? I am really not interested in the names or personal information on any of the clients, but only on the frequency of visits, costs of procedures, and trying to piece together an accurate prediction of the lost revenues of this office for the days until we staff it with a new surgeon. I would be willing to wait while you copy his files and white-out all the personal information if that would make you more comfortable."

I could see she considered the enormous task it would be for her to white out all personal information and decided to throw caution to the wind in an effort to secure her future employment. She accepted that these were unusual circumstances that dictated giving someone access to these files. Without Jack to dictate to her who should have access to these files, it was now left up to her to decide. Seeing me as her potential savior in regards to her financial future, she elected to give me access to these files. But having been trained well by Jack she quickly produced a non-disclosure agreement for me to sign.

Stella led me to Jack's office and started to unlock the door, but it swung open as she started to push the key into the lock.

"Does Jack usually leave his office unlocked?" I asked Stella.

"No, but he was in a rush to get out of here last Friday to make his plane so I'm sure he just didn't pull it all the way shut." she replied. Stella returned to her desk to replace the key.

Jack's office was a mixture of formality you would expect from a reputed doctor's office. Oak desk, filing cabinets, chrome fixtures mixed with the casual décor I remember Jack for in our teen years when I used to hang out with him in his bedroom. While gazing about the room my eyes fell upon the basketball with Magic Johnson's autograph displayed on top of one of his bookcase. I approached the ball and fell into a trance remembering the Los Angeles Laker's game I attended with Jack when he received that autograph. Stella re-entered the room with Jack's filing cabinet keys and startled me.

"Jack was very proud of that ball." Stella commented.

I had an almost uncontrollable urge to tell her that I was with Jack when he got that autograph. It was one of the unforgettable memories I had of my youthful days with Jack and I had to regain my composure with Stella in the room. After all, I was supposed to be a detached bystander not having any personal relationship with Jack.

Not wanting to appear suspicious by looking for one specific file, I pulled a chair over to the first filing cabinet labeled A-F and opened my briefcase and set it on top. I pulled out my legal pad and pen, and then inserted Jack's key and unlocked the first drawer. I started to just count the number of hanging files and make some notes on my pad without actually removing any files from the drawer, but I was basically just biding time while Stella was watching me from the doorway. Eventually, the phone rang and Stella left me alone to my task at hand. I quickly moved over to the drawer marked 'S' and inserted Jack's key. There must have been 50 hanging folders in this one drawer, and out of curiosity I quietly calculated in my head how much money Jack must have earned from the clients he had in just this one drawer alone. I then perused the folders and came across one empty hanging folder near the very back. The hanging folders themselves did not have any names marked on them but the files inside did have conspicuously marked names on the upper left-hand corner of each cover. I opened the folder in front of the empty folder and noticed that it held a file for a Ms. Julia Swanson. I then opened the folder after the empty folder and noted that it contained a file for a Mr. George Sylvan. I got a very eerie feeling at that point. This was much too unsettling to be a coincidence. If I filed any paperwork alphabetically for a Jeremiah Sweinstein it would fit conveniently into the empty folder. Nervously and quickly I checked several other drawers. It seems Jack was very meticulous and only added new hanging folders as he added new client files and the empty folder between Swanson and Sylvan was the only empty folder in all of his drawers. I looked around his office but didn't find any stash of empty folders. But I did find a stash of empty folders in the last drawer labeled X-Z. I considered asking Stella to unlock Jack's desk to see if Jack had any client information locked up there but then reconsidered since I really needed to keep my cover story valid if I needed to return to Jack's office later. Access to Jack's desk might be pushing Stella's assistance to the limit and I couldn't come up with a valid reason for rifling through his desk at this point.

I returned to Stella to ask her a few questions about security.

"Stella, where does Jack normally keep his key to the filing cabinets? Security is not necessarily the purpose of my visit, but I would be remiss in my duties to Lloyds if I didn't verify a few basic requirements." I asked.

"The key I gave you is my personal key. I keep it locked in my bottom drawer of my desk. I am the one who unlocks Jack's files every morning before he comes in and locks them at night before I leave. Jack has his own key that he uses to lock the cabinets in the event that I leave before him, but I'm fairly sure he keeps it on his key ring with his car and house key." She responded.

"And you locked them up Friday after Jack left?" I asked her.

"Yes Sir" she responded. "I didn't unlock them this morning because I knew Jack would not be in."

An uncomfortable silence followed so I quickly returned to Jack's office. I decided to do a closer inspection of the drawer that would have contained Sweinstein's file. It appeared that the drawer hinge was slightly askew. I notice some barely perceptible marks between the drawer and the cabinet and having jimmied a few filing cabinets myself I recognized this to be the ideal spot to put a screwdriver if you wanted access to the internals without the keys.

I spent another 10 minutes in Jack's office before I came to the conclusion I was fresh out of additional clues. It was apparent someone had pilfered the file Jack had created for his mysterious visitor. I pulled out my notes that I had jotted down about Jack's practice the previous night. Then I realized the startling discovery of the jimmied file drawer had distracted me from the second important task I had planned for this visit. I returned to the office doorway to address Stella again.

"Stella, I'm seeing a vast difference in the practice's income per client based on the type of procedure performed. I already have Jack's standard fee list from our insurance files, but don't have a good feel for a typical ratio of his high cost procedures compared to his lower costs procedures. Are you able to print out a breakdown of Jack's cases by type of procedure so I can more accurately estimate his average income per week?"

"Yes Sir I can." She responded.

"Can I see that list for the last 12 months? Jack has already submitted last years to our office, but it's possible his average procedure costs has increased since then."

Stella popped in a few keys on her computer keyboard, and the printer came to life. After Stella handed me the stack I returned to Jack's office to examine the print-out. I was only interested in one procedure. Pete had mentioned that Jack had performed breast enlargement on the woman accusing him of making unwanted advancements. Jack had only performed three breast enhancement procedures in the last 12 months. I poked my head out of the office to ask Stella if this was an unusually short list for this particularly common procedure. Stella explained that Jack's clients fit into two basic categories. One being those with severe disfigurations that came to Jack because of his new innovative procedures and his high success rate and the other being those that came to him for 'routine' services that were willing to pay many times the normal fee for Jack's discretion and expertise. It seems that breast enhancement is such a routine procedure nowadays that most clients would take that business to a less expensive surgeon. I returned to the filing cabinet to extract the three files for breast enhancement and then retired to Jack's comfortable leather chair (I must get one of these for my office I pondered) to look over his cases. The first case last November involved a Duchess from England. Looking at her age and the status of her family I found it hard to believe Jack would have pursued a relationship with this woman. The second procedure (5 months ago) involved a fairly famous Hollywood movie star that if I remembered correctly was married to her producer a month prior to her surgery. I'm guessing the procedure was a wedding present to her husband more so than a career enhancement procedure. The third procedure, only one month ago was a name I did not recognize. Gloria Jansen. I noticed she had a local address here in Chicago and by process of elimination it appears I had found the woman Jack was supposed to have committed suicide over. Jack's files seemed to contain only the minimum information necessary to facilitate the actual procedure and billing so I was unable to determine if this was in fact the girl that Pete refused to discuss with me. I made a few more notes in my notebook and then packed up all my materials and closed Jack's office door as I returned to the lobby. I returned Jack's filing cabinet keys to Stella and informed her that I had all the information I needed to accurately calculate the lost income claims of his associates.

"Stella, do you mind giving me a quick tour of his lab so I can jot down a few notes concerning his inventory and security?"

"Not at all Mr. Miles, follow me."

Yellow notepad in hand I proceeded to randomly jot down facts and figures on it while making sure to keep Stella from being able to see that

I was just writing nonsense. After appearing to finish up my inventory I calculated the best way to ask the next question.

"Stella, when Jack performed a lab test in here, such as say a blood test, how does he keep record of who it was for? Did he have to go back to his filing cabinets in his office to record his results? I just ask to verify he isn't jeopardizing his clients confidentiality by keeping unlocked records here."

"Jack does keep an unlocked log in here to record those findings but he records it by file number and not by any personal information."

"Where would that log be?"

"He keeps it right over here by the sample refrigerator...., well that's strange, I don't see his log. He always keeps it right here by his sample cooler. I can keep an eye out for it and contact you when I find it if you need to look at it?"

"That won't be necessary Stella. I just needed to make sure it didn't violate Jack's confidentiality agreements. "

I casually walked over to the sample refrigerator and opened it for a quick peek. I intentionally positioned my body between Stella and the refrigerator because if my suspicions were valid, I did not want to alarm Stella. Inside I could see a metal tray that appeared to be the holder for the blood samples. As I suspected though, it was empty.

I was now convinced that Mr. Sweinstein's thugs had returned to Jack's office to not only retrieve his file, but to also erase any record of his blood test. Assuming the blood samples did not have any labels identifying which was Mr. Sweinstein's, it appears they elected to just take them all.

As I left the lab with Stella following behind I opened my briefcase and put the yellow notepad in.

"Thank you for all your help Stella. I should have all the information I need to process the claim. Will you be here later today or tomorrow if I should need to gather more information?"

"Well. Jack's attorney called me this morning before you came in to tell me to cancel all of Jack's appointments. He also told me to continue to man the office and answer the phones but not to give out any information concerning Jack other than to say we would not be scheduling any new appointments. He said he would be back to me before the end of the week once he knew better what to do with Jack's office. I should probably have him talk to you about the insurance claim. Let me give him a call now."

For the inexperienced undercover agent this might have created some panic. Quick thinking for situations such as this were becoming routine for me by this time.

"Actually Stella, I've already spoken with him briefly today and I am planning on stopping by his office again tomorrow. Just follow whatever instructions he has given to you and we will inform you when we have something firm about rescheduling appointments. I'm sorry if I came off as too professional concerning this sad situation. I understand you might have been very close to Mr. Lambert so please accept my sympathy with your situation. I assure you that we will process this all as soon as we can and try and get you back to a normal routine in the near future."

I figured this might give me enough time for another visit to Jack's office later this evening or tomorrow morning before Stella talks to Jack's attorney again if the need arose. On the off chance that Stella does call Jack's attorney and he does get suspicious I would have to keep a close eye on Stella reaction if I did stop by again to see if she has been alerted to my charade. If I do have to return to the office, and it appears Stella is on to me, I will have to have a quick escape route set up prior to my visit since I'm sure my fraudulent presentation and access to Jack's files would raise an eyebrow not only with Jack's attorney and associates but also with the local police.

After leaving Jack's office I returned to my hotel room and spent the next hour looking into Gloria Jansen. I was able to ascertain that she was a fairly successful model. While the breast enhancement might fall in line with her career it didn't necessarily fall in line with Pete's mentioning her breast enhancement possibly impacting on her career. After all, I would assume this sort of procedure would be common place now for modeling. I attributed Gloria's desire for Pete to keep her name out of the press associated with Jack's death to be a little more of a criminal concern than an employment concern.

It was time to look further into exactly who Gloria Jansen was. At this point I considered her to be an accessory to murder and that she would not be very likely to open up to questioning. But I had already prepared my angle before even leaving for Chicago. I had acquired her address and phone number from her file. I pulled out my Go-Phone and gave Gloria a call. It would be preferential to leave as little evidence as possible that could lead them to me, such as Gloria using caller ID to identify me through my cell phone or hotel room phone. After four rings I was beginning to believe I would be transferred to voicemail, but then she answered with a soft sultry voice.

"Hello Gloria? My name is George Durham. I'm a modeling scout for Victoria's Secret and we're doing some preliminary legwork in regards to a new line of cosmetics coming out soon. Our office has you down on our list of those we should consider for one of our cover girls for this new cosmetic line. Would you be interested in this opportunity? " I asked.

"I believe I would." She replied

"I was wondering if I could do a preliminary interview with you as a potential candidate?" I asked.

"Victoria's Secret you say? It does sound very interesting but I wasn't even aware that Victoria's Secret had their own cosmetic line."

"It's something new we are planning to come out with in about 4 months. Would you be interested in a quick preliminary interview today? It won't take more than about 10 minutes if you can spare the time."

"I currently have a tight calendar, but I wouldn't mind listening to what you have to offer. When would you like to do this?" she replied.

"I've just completed one interview near you and had you on my list as a potential interview if I have the time before my departing flight."

I was trying to put together a story line indicating this would be her one and only chance for this opportunity.

"I'm in the neighborhood if you have any openings this morning?" I asked.

"I was just getting ready to head out to a prior engagement. How long did you say it would take?" she replied.

"I'm only doing preliminary candidate screening right now involving looking at your dossiers, discussing backgrounds, checking any possible conflicting contracts, the what-not. I don't anticipate this initial process taking more than 10 minutes, if you pass my initial screening we would want to set up a much longer interview with you in the near future with our head talent scout. Basically we want to make sure there aren't any show-stoppers with our candidates. After we narrow down our list to those that could actually fill the position we will schedule a full blown employment interview down at our corporate office. Would you consider letting me stop by for a quick meeting this morning?"

"Well, I've got a shoot coming up at noon, so I don't have very long. You say this will only take about 10 minutes? How long would it take you to get here? I live at the Livingston Penthouses on the waterfront."

"I'm just around the corner. It's just an initial screening process to preclude a bigger waste of your time if you don't meet our pre-requisites. I can be at your place within 5 minutes if that's okay with you."

There was a pause and I was worried I had blown it with my pushiness and saying I could be at her place in 5 minutes. Then she responded:

"I can meet you down in the lobby in 10 minutes Mr. Durham."

This would work. I figured her caution at wanting to meet me in the lobby was out of concern for my legitimacy but as long as I can get her to answer a few questions I was okay with that.

Gloria's penthouse apartment building was indicative of a wealthy lifestyle. The doorman let me in when I informed him that Gloria would be meeting me in the lobby but he had some quiet words with the front desk attendant which I assume was to caution him to keep an eye on me that I didn't slip up the stairs or elevator. I can only assume that paparazzi or over zealous fans might want to visit a few of the more prominent residences and the staff was trained to protect the privacy of their tenants. The lobby was decorated with numerous floor to ceiling mirrors so I took the opportunity to look myself over and judge just how much I looked like a modeling talent scout. I double-checked my business card was handy in my breast pocket and then as I did some last minute tugs on my lapel and collar the elevator dinged.

Gloria was stunning. But I needed to maintain my composure as a scout who would no doubt see this type of beauty on a daily basis. I was starting to have my doubts about whether Jack would stick to his policy of not having a relationship with a client after seeing what Gloria looked like.

"Gloria? George Durham here. It's so nice to meet you." I could see apprehension in her eyes so I quickly pulled out my business card and presented it to her as I shook her hand.

"Nice to meet you too George. I'm surprised that Victoria's Secret is expanding into cosmetics."

"It's been in the works for over a year now and they would like to have the perfect face to present the line with when they debut it."

"I am honored that they would consider me. What type of information did you need today?" I could see the apprehension rapidly being replaced by aspiration and optimism. Greed has always been one of the most useful tools in the Private Detective's bag of tools for extracting information from strangers.

"Well, the first show-stopper would be any exclusive contracts you might have with other companies that might preclude you being the 'face' we want people to come to know as the Victoria's face for cosmetics."

"I mostly free-lance Mr. Durham. However, I do have a contract with

Dubois Cosmetics out of Paris, but it is not exclusive. Even though I have been with them for three years now, it is a year to year contract that would require renewal in August. I would be open to the idea of not renewing my contract with Dubois if Victoria's Secret decides I'm their girl."

"That is acceptable." I responded. "A second potential show-stopper would be if our competitors leaked it out that our models were actually beautiful for artificial reasons beyond our cosmetics. We would like our customers to believe that our cosmetics were the sole reason for our model's beauty. While we are not necessarily stating we cannot use a model that has had cosmetic enhancements we would like to know up front what those enhancements might be so we can evaluate if it could be a embarrassment in the future. I apologize for asking this personal question but it is pertinent to our selection process Gloria."

"No apologies necessary Mr. Durham. My face is untouched by cosmetic surgery though I have had a very slight breast enhancement and the removal of two moles on my left shoulder. Other than that, what you see is all me George."

I sensed a slight flirt here. I must maintain my composure since it was obvious she was interested in the Victoria modeling position and not me personally. My guess would be that turning on the charm was a natural part of a model's career when talking to potential talent scouts.

"Mole removal is routine and shouldn't be a concern. Since the majority of our cosmetic line is geared towards the face, the breast enhancement also shouldn't be a problem, but since our commercials would still portray the 'entire' Victoria's girl we would still prefer to keep that information to ourselves. The discretion of your doctor might be of concern here since it is not unheard of for the tabloids to pay doctors to exaggerate what they had done for their more prominent patients."

"Not a concern Mr. Durham. My procedure was done by Dr. Jack Lambert. If you check him out you will find him to be one of the most renowned and discreet cosmetic surgeons available in the country."

"Ah yes, the one who was in the news for falling to his death from a hotel balcony in Los Angeles recently. We've actually sent a few of our models to him for some minor facial imperfections so I was shocked to hear about this. While slight facial alterations wouldn't be a concern for our models representing our lingerie line, it might be inappropriate for someone representing our cosmetics line. So it's good to hear your face is untouched by surgery. I'm sure you understand when our product professes to be responsible for facial beauty itself we must be unimpeachable on that statement."

It was time to fish for a little reaction.

"It was disappointing to hear that Dr. Lambert fell to his death in Los Angeles. Did you hear anything about that?"

I could see obvious discomfort in Gloria regarding this question.

"Yes, I did see that in the news. It's tragic. He was the best in his field."

I looked for any other chinks in her composure, and as I looked, it appeared a tad bit of her apprehension about talking to me might have resurfaced. I glanced down as my notes again to try and halt that apprehension. I quickly gauged my next question. But it was all or nothing at this point. My whole masquerade was based the next piece of information I was hoping to elicit from her. If I left at this point I really gained nothing from this interview.

"The last show stopper I need to ask you about is likely the most sensitive and personal. But this question is essential in our initial screening process. This would involve your reputation. While our line has already performed a criminal background check on all our potential cover girls there might always be those hidden skeletons that pop up. You understand that Victoria's Secret has a much higher standard and reputation than all of our competitors, and we value it and guard it with extreme care. If there is anything in your background that could negatively impact you representing the Victoria line just tell me you are not interested in this position and I will walk away with no questions asked. The Victoria's "Angel" concept is one we would not wish to tarnish so I do not limit this request to illegal activities. Any kind of substance abuse legal or otherwise would nullify your eligibility for this position. Anything the public would consider to be unethical could also jeopardize your eligibility. We would also need to know if you have been or are currently involved in any type of scandal or affair whether it is public or not. If there is something in your past or present you feel would jeopardize your being the face we are looking for, you can simply ask us to not consider you as a candidate and we will not pry any further. But if you would still like us to consider you for this position you must be upfront and honest in this matter. If you answered no to this question and we pursued a contract with you only to find out later there was something you did not disclose you could be liable for damages to the Victoria name. You do understand the importance of these questions don't you Gloria?"

"Yes. I've been through this before Mr. Durham."

"I'm sorry if these questions come off as intimidating, but protecting Victoria's Secret's name is a major objective of our initial screening interview. You don't have to share anything with me that you wish to keep private. But if there is something that you are unsure of, just give me a non-detailed synopsis of the situation and I can tell you whether or not it would preclude our using you as a model."

I was free to scrutinize Gloria's expression at this point without hurting my cover. A scout would most certainly evaluate any suspicious response from Gloria at this point so I was free to intensely watch her eyes to see if that apprehension returned or whether she appeared to be worried over not being considered for a catapulting career move. My cover was based on my maintaining eye-contact through the course of her answering this question.

She was hard to read. In one split second it looked like she was going to bounce me out the door and then she regained her composure and thought carefully as she answered.

"There is one small thing that has just occurred that will most likely never become public. But on the off-hand it does can I share it with you under the strictest confidentiality?" she asked.

"I can assure you Gloria that any information that you share with me would be maintained with the utmost confidentiality regardless of your eligibility for this position." I responded.

"The potential exists that Jack Lambert committed suicide due to my rejecting his advances."

"I thought the news report said it was an accident?" I replied.

I feigned ignorance about the suicide aspect of the news report in an attempt to get it to appear more like it was Gloria's idea to elaborate rather than her responding to my questioning the circumstances of Jack's death.

"I believe they are presenting it to the press as either being an accident or a suicide. I can't say for sure that I am the reason that he committed suicide, but he made repeated advancements to me including a phone call shortly before his death. I did absolutely nothing inappropriate and my relationship with him was strictly professional."

"Who knows about this Gloria? Victoria's could not become part to withholding information from the police."

"The police do know about it Mr. Durham. They came and questioned me shortly after his death."

"What led them to question you on this?"

"Jack's phone records show that he called me just a few short minutes before he jumped to his death. He made another attempt to get me to go out on a date with him. I politely asked him to stop his advances and explained that there just was no chance of me starting a relationship with him. I really had no idea he would be suicidal over this."

"But you've been up front and honest with the police on this, right? I mean, you didn't do anything wrong to lead him on that the public would frown on if they knew did you?"

"Oh no! Not at all. He just kept calling me from home, from work and where ever he happened to be. I tried to decline him politely, but he persisted. I had no idea he was taking it so hard. The police assured me that they would treat me similar to that of a victim of a stalker and keep my name out of the press if possible."

"Well I'm sure all models experience unwanted advances. We have some time before they narrow the list to the final few. I'm sure if there was anything negative to come out on this it would happen before that point. I thank you for being upfront about this. I'm fairly confident this will not negatively affect our considering you for the position unless something other than what you have said comes to light. If the police approach you about this again would it be possible for you to update me with any additional information you might believe pertinent to your reputation? While I am just a scout, the agency does take my personal recommendations seriously and I will write up the Dr. Lambert issue as not being a disqualifier."

"Thank you Mr. Durham. I will give you a call if anything further develops concerning Dr. Lambert." she said with a broad smile on her face. She glanced at my business card to ensure it had a phone number.

"Well okay then Gloria. You have my card. I will get back to you within a week to let you know how the screening process is going. I can't make any promises because I don't have the final say. But even though you were just a tentative interview I am impressed by your facial features and plan to put in a very favorable recommendation to my superiors."

Gloria beamed at this point. A final comment to instill optimism can do wonders to subdue suspicions that might arise later.

We shook hands and I left. I didn't expect to receive any new information from Gloria but on the off-chance she did decide to reveal anything else I had purchased an untraceable Go-Phone back in L.A. for this trip to Chicago and that number was on the business card I gave to Gloria as we introduced ourselves.

Unfortunately the interview with Gloria didn't provide me with any holes in Pete's suicide scenario but it did provide me with a bit of information that Pete didn't share with me. Gloria stated that Jack called her repeatedly from his office and home. No doubt she would assume that I had no method to disprove this and maybe she didn't share this information with Pete knowing he would undoubtedly be able to verify its validity. My gut was telling me that even though Gloria's story was no doubt fictitious she would feel obligated to paint Jack's death as being a one-sided infatuation to keep from blowing her potential deal with Victoria's Secret. When I returned to my hotel room I decided to check out the validity of Gloria's story. A quick phone call is all that was needed.

"Central Intelligence Agency, how may I direct your call?" The person at the other end answered.

"Extension 4384 please." I responded.

A second or two went by then the transfer was answered.

"State your name and security code please." The female voice on the other end asked.

"Jordan Gaites. 934565, security code 'Morning Glory'." I responded.

There was about a 30 second silence while the person at the other end verified my identity.

"Good afternoon Mr. Gaites. How may I be of assistance?" she asked.

"I need last month's phone records for both a cell phone and business phone."

Another pause while the person at the other end evaluated my request.

"Mr. Gaites, I show that you are no longer active with the agency." She responded.

"Yes, that is true, but if I'm not mistaken, I retained the ability to access these services on a limited basis when needed. I believe you will find that I have never abused this service."

"I see that you have not utilized this service at all since your discharge." She acknowledged. "Please give me the phone numbers you would like accessed and in what manner you would like to receive the records."

I gave the agent both Jacks cell phone number and office phone number along with my personal email address and then ended the conversation. Within an hour I had Jack's home and office phone records in my email inbox. As I suspected, there was no record of any calls to Gloria's phone other than a single call from the office back at the time of her procedure. I thought of going to Pete with this information but realized it would probably only get me counseled once again about letting the police do their job. It would only be Gloria's word against mine concerning her statement about the phone calls and probably set myself up for a fraud lawsuit concerning the method in which I obtained information from Gloria. It would also be awkward explain to the police how I acquired Jack's phone records. I didn't see much more that I would be able to pursue here in Chicago so I planned on using one of the three return trip reservations I had made prior to leaving Los Angeles. I called to cancel the other two reservations but kept the reservation for the next morning. I was a little disappointed in myself for not have scheduled one for this evening, but I didn't anticipate getting all the information I did in such a short time. I needed the rest anyways and decided to spend one more night in my hotel room. This gave me the rest of the evening to see what else I could find on the internet of use in my investigation. A good place to start would be Gloria's current employer, Dubois Cosmetics. A quick Google produced:

Dubois Cosmetics: Lots of information on the internet about Dubois Cosmetics. While the Paris based cosmetic line was very popular it was a little know fact that it was in fact a subsidiary of Fracious Cosmetics…, owned by Joseph DeLoreon.

CHAPTER 4
JACK'S ASSOCIATES

THE REVELATION OF GLORIA BEING an employee of Joseph DeLoreon bothered me so much that I got almost no sleep that last night in the hotel. I no longer had any doubts that the DeLoreon Foundation and Gloria Jansen were somehow involved in Jack's death but still didn't have enough evidence to take to the police. It was too much of a coincidence she was employed by the same company responsible for a mysterious visit to Jack two nights before his death and that she lied to me about Jack repeatedly calling her on the phone. Other than my suspicions about Gloria there was no proof anyone from the DeLoreon Foundation even visited Jack at his office the afternoon before his death. And even if I could convince Pete that Jack did have a mysterious visitor from the DeLoreon Foundation he would probably say it was just a coincidence that Gloria was employed by them. Or he might say that DeLoreon's interest in Jack's research was the specific reason Gloria was sent to him for her surgery but in no way would implicate them in his death. I needed a motive. Jack's research must certainly be worth a lot of money to the medical world. Maybe Jack shared with Gloria about his research back when she had her breast enhancement and she shared that information with Joseph DeLoreon. Or maybe Gloria's visit was scheduled in advance to set up a cover story for Jack's suicide.

Paul Eckert, one of Jack's associates, had an office in Los Angeles only twelve miles from my home and would be my next stop. My flight out of Chicago ended up being delayed 2 hours, so I spent some more time on their WiFi looking into Jack's research. But being that he and his associates had not publicly announced the results of their research yet, very little was available on the internet concerning new innovations in plastic surgery on minor scars. And none of what I could find was linked to Jack or his associates. Lack of sleep started catching up with me and I decided to catch a little nap on the flight back home, but even that was interrupted by a couple with an unruly infant child sitting behind me. It was still morning when I arrived back in Los Angeles due to the time zone change, so I decided to grab a few hours' sleep at home before giving Paul Eckert a call. I was able to talk to Paul directly and for once it seemed the best approach was the honest one.

"Hello Mr. Eckert? This is Jordan Gaites. I am a close personal friend of Jack Lambert's and was wondering if you had the time to talk to me. I have some serious reservations about the news story concerning his death and was hoping you would let me share them with you."

"This is Jordy?" Paul asked.

I was a little surprised that not only had he heard of me, but that he addressed me by the nickname that Jack used for me.

"Yes it it. I take it that Jack has mentioned me to you?" I asked.

"On several occasions." He responded. "By all means, let's talk. I also am confused about the reports and have questions of my own."

"I can be by this afternoon if that's okay?" I asked.

"I have an opening at 3 p.m. if that's okay with you." He responded.

"That will be fine. Do you need directions to my office?" Paul asked.

"I can find my way, see you at three." I responded.

Paul's office was similar to Jack's in function but the décor was significantly more staunch and professional. Jack's practice mostly focused on facial procedures while Paul was more into body enhancements. Liposuction and implants seemed to make up the majority of his procedures based upon the various posters and props visible in his lobby. I announced to Paul's receptionist who I was and Paul immediately stuck his head out of his office.

"Jordy! I hope you don't mind me calling you that? It's just that Jack never referred to you by any other name." Paul exclaimed while motioning me back to his office.

"Not at all." I said, though it really was a little unsettling having a total stranger call me that.

"It's good to finally meet you though I am so sorry for the circumstances." He said as he indicated for me wait a second. Paul then stuck his head back out of his office door and told his receptionist he did not wish to be disturbed for 10-15 minutes and asked that she tell his next client when they arrived that he would be with them shortly. He then motioned for me to follow him and escorted me to a room next to his office that I assumed was where he conferred with his clients with what he might be able to do for them. The room was much less sterile than the rest of his clinic and the décor was intent on putting the client at ease about the medical procedures they were considering undertaking. If you didn't know you were in a doctor's clinic you would swear you were in the comfortable den of Paul's private residence. The booklets on the coffee table depicting pictures of the various medical procedures Paul performed were the only items in the room that were slightly out of place with their surroundings.

"Have a seat Jordy." Paul directed me to a plush couch on one side of the coffee table and he sat down in a wing chair on the other side.

"Thank you for taking time out to talk with me on such a short notice." I replied.

"Jack's other associates and I were shocked to hear of his death and we are at a loss as to why Jack might commit suicide."

"That's why I'm here Mr. Eckert. I'm not sure what all Jack may have told you about me but private investigation is my specialty and I really would like to get to the bottom of what happened to Jack. I don't believe Jack committed suicide at all and I'm looking into the possibility that he was murdered by someone interested in his new research into skin-melding."

"How so? And please call me Paul." He responded.

With a raised eyebrow I could see the concern in Paul's eyes. After all, he and Jack were partners on this endeavor and if their research was something that would get Jack killed, most certainly he would be concerned for his own safety.

I explained the police investigator's theory of Jack being despondent over Gloria's rejection having driven him to suicide. Paul agreed wholeheartedly with me that this did not sound like Jack at all. I could now see Paul shared my intense interest in the real reason for Jack's death, even though our motivation for this interest differed significantly.

I shared Jack's story of his office visit two nights before his death and explained the intense interest this man had in the skin-melding procedure and the secretive nature of his visit. Paul then shared with me a similar mysterious visit he had the week prior to Jack's death concerning their research.

"A gentleman showed up in my office unannounced and wanted to know if I was performing the skin-melding procedure on any clients. I told him the procedure was still in the testing phase and only being performed by one of my associates under strict trial phase rules and guidelines. I asked him where he had heard about the procedure considering we had not published any results yet. The gentleman stopped his questions at that point and left abruptly. It seems he really wasn't so interested in details of the process but only on whether I could perform it. As soon as he found out I did not perform the procedure he went upon his merry way. My visitor was not nearly as mysterious as the one you describe that visited Jack though. It was a single solitary man with no facial scars or cloak and dagger arrival scenario. He was middle aged, wearing a suit and tie and did not share any specific information regarding the reason for his interest in our new technique. "

I then explained to Paul about my findings about the DeLoreon Foundation and the relationship between that visitor and Gloria. I left out the part about my deceptive entrance into Jack's personal files believing that Paul might not look on this favorably being a discreet surgeon himself. Considering Paul and Jack shared many of the same clients I believed that was also a good reason for not sharing my indiscretions at Jack's office. Paul just assumed I got my information about Gloria from my police connections. I went into detail about DeLoreon's interest in cosmetics and cosmetic surgery and the possible link between that interest and the research that Paul and Jack were working on.

At this point I suggested to Paul that I believed the DeLoreon Foundation might be after Jack's research and that large profits might be the motive. Paul shook his head slowly and informed me that this could not possibly be the case.

"Why, isn't the potential profit from this procedure enormous?" I asked.

"It's like this Jordy. The skin-melding therapy process is not a secret that can be stolen anymore. We just published all information concerning the actual mechanics involved in several medical journals that will be released next week. Jack was scheduled to release the positive results we are seeing in our test subjects at last weekend's conference to prepare the medical field for the information they would see in the upcoming journals. Anyone planning to steal technology successfully would need to do so prior to public release of it. The whole world will become aware of the process upon the release of those journals. Hopefully it will be a procedure practiced in cosmetic surgery offices world-wide within the next few years."

"I don't understand." I replied. "How could you possibly profit from this research if you have shared it with everyone else?" I asked.

"We own the patent to the chemical concoction used to make the skin and sub-tissues pliable." Paul replied. "Jack, myself and our other two associates share the patent on this. While anyone could take our research and develop their own version of the equipment to make it work, if they were to try and market or profit from our procedure they would be violating our chemical copyright. We could sue. Any practice wishing to use this procedure will be required to pay us royalties for the use of the chemicals. Our partnership is no secret and even if the DeLoreon Foundation decided to knock all four of us off in the hopes of stealing our copyright it wouldn't work. I really don't see where they could possibly benefit from Jack's death. Jack's share of the patent was willed back to the partnership, so there isn't even an heir that would have benefited from his death in terms of this patent. Certainly if any of his other three associates were to meet an untimely demise the authorities would have to get suspicious and launch an investigation. For partners such as myself who have heirs, in the untimely event of my death my share of the patent is willed to my wife and kids."

"Has anyone approached you concerning the sale of your process? Could Jack have been killed because he resisted pressure to sell his portion of the patent?"

"No one has approached me concerning selling our patent, and to my knowledge no one has approached any of the other associates concerning this. If someone did kill Jack because he didn't want to sell the patent his share of the patent is now split between the other three associates. I believe any potential buyer would find that none of us has any desire to sell this procedure. I don't believe anyone outside the cosmetic surgeon world would recognize the value of the procedure as much as us. We would have to be insane to sell this procedure at this point in its development. This procedure means much more to us than just profit. Our work is like art to us and this procedure will dramatically change the limitations of what we are allowed to do with our art. "

This threw an enormous monkey wrench into my theory of the motive behind Jack's death. My line of questioning at this point was stonewalled. As I was trying to think of any further questions I might have for Paul he seemed to shift uncomfortably in his chair and then began to speak again.

"The only one who may have profited slightly from Jack's death is the three of us who will now split his share of the patent. But you must understand Mr. Gaites that we are all very anxious to get the procedure through the testing phase. Jack's death will create a serious setback in our planned release date for this procedure. All of us are already independently wealthy and while we may eventually profit from Jack's death we all have much more to lose in the immediate future by Jack's death than we do to gain by it. I believe that I speak for my associates when I say that the prestige we will all get from the release of this procedure is more important that the monetary gain, and right now that release has been put on hold due to Jack's unfortunate death prior to his presentation at the convention."

"I am sorry if I made you feel uncomfortable with my theory about Jack being murdered Paul. I in no way suspect any of his associates as being involved. Are there any serious side effects with the technique? Could it be that Jack's procedure failed miserably on this patient and the motive for his death could be revenge?" I asked. I know I was probably way off on this speculation, but hoped that maybe Paul could come up with a motive.

"Doubtful." Paul responded. "Jack was the one performing the testing because of his expertise in facial surgery and our anticipation is that this will be the primary use of this procedure. Of all the various cosmetic surgeries available today, those done on the face are the ones that require the most caution. Paul's procedures typically require a lot more finesse that the ones I perform and he limited his testing of the technique to very small areas not normally visible on the off chance there was a negative reaction. Jack has been testing the procedure on other patients for months with no adverse side-effects. From what you've told me it sounds like this person had more appearance concerns before Jack's procedure than he could possibly encounter after Jack worked on him. We are exploring long-term side effects, but from what you've said, Jack was murdered less than 24 hours after performing the procedure on this gentleman."

I exhausted all I could think of to ask Paul and realized he was delaying his next appointment while we talked. So I thanked Paul for talking with me and promised to keep in touch with him should I uncover any new information about Jack's death.

I returned home to regroup and decide if I was in a stalemate regarding my investigation. I decided to contact Jack's other associates via telephone instead of visiting them in person since I was not optimistic about gathering any new information. It seems the gentleman that visited Paul might also have visited one of Jack's other two associates. But as in the case of Paul's visit, the gentleman shared no information at all about himself or the reason for his inquiry. At some point in his inquiries the gentleman must have found out that Jack was performing the procedure because the visit to Jack's office by the scarred older man was much more than just an information gathering visit by a single person as in the previous two visits to Jack's associates.

Both associates also expressed their disbelief in the theory that Jack might have committed suicide. Other than echoing Paul's doubt about theft being a motive, the other associates provided no useful information.

Chapter 5

The Deloreon Mystery

HAVING FELT I HAD REACHED a dead end in my theory about the theft of Jack's research being a motive I decided to set aside my investigation into Jack's new medical technique and decided to focus more on The DeLoreon Foundation and Gloria Jansen. I could think of no threads to pull on to unravel my mystery so I had hopes that shot-gunning for information about the two might eventually give me a new lead. Without a motive I was hard pressed to prove they had any connection to Jack's death. While my research supported the fact that Gloria was a successful model I could find nothing out of the ordinary about her personal life or career. I pasted together a history of her from high school to her present position with Dubois Cosmetics. It appeared that everything was as she stated in my interview with her. She first became employed with Dubois three years earlier when she did a photo shoot in France for a not so popular fashion magazine. I exhausted a whole evening finding information about Gloria including every resource I could find, some legit, some not so legit. While Gloria had been picked up by the police once at the age of 17 for shoplifting the charges were dropped and she has had no run-in's with the law ever since. I developed the opinion that Gloria was simply a pawn of the DeLoreon foundation and that I could not progress my investigation any further by focusing on her.

Joseph DeLoreon's background proved much more difficult to research than Gloria's. Partly because his citizenship was in the Bahamas and both he and his father John had been tycoon recluses their whole life. The DeLoreon family owned an island called North Cat Cay in the

Bahamas since before the earliest recorded real estate records I could find for the Bahamas in the mid 1800's. Joseph's father poured large sums of money into a mansion on the island and protected his privacy with a large security force. I exhausted all my usual legal research methods trying to find information about Joseph. Having lost my lifelong friend to what I believed to be murder I decided to risk my somewhat clean record and pursue a few of my not so legal methods available to me for background investigations. I had an upper hand on most Private Investigators with my CIA experience and connections. But up until this point I had rarely put to use the majority of my acquired talents. I no longer had the backing of the United States Government for any covert endeavors I might undertake and I was therefore risking prosecution and prison time should I be caught doing things I was free to do on a daily basis in the past with immunity. Since leaving the CIA, utilizing that which I learned while there had been limited to counterfeiting identity documents and a few other non-risky spook devices used for recording audio or video. The majority of my document counterfeiting was business cards, letterheads and the what-not, but I occasionally popped out various ID cards to gain access to needed information in my investigations. But it was time to go deep undercover for my future investigative plans for Jack's murder. I went to a few sources I had not used since my CIA days to acquire a new untraceable laptop, wireless gadgets and several items that I may or may not utilize in the next coming weeks. I also contacted one of my computer hacking friends to look into DeLoreon's private financial transactions. I hesitated to use my official connection that I used for Jack's phone records thinking that I should save that for a situation when I had no other alternatives. Through my personal source I was able to track numerous contractor renovations, improvements and security systems installed on North Cat Cay Island. I was also able to identify a recent transfer of $50,000 to a newly opened Bahamas account that ultimately proved to be linkable to Gloria Jansen. But once again this was evidence that I would never be able to present to the police because of my methods for acquiring it. But it did show me that Gloria had been paid off for her part in covering up Jack's death.

That was about the extent of useful financial dealings I could find and the rest provided nothing I could link to Jack's death. Joseph never utilized public transportation but I could trace his whereabouts based on certain purchases and recorded flight plans for his private helicopters and Lear jets. He had very expensive taste in food, clothes and lodging that I could use to place his whereabouts and even though this one tidbit of information placed him in Chicago for his appointment with Jack, it did not put him in Los Angeles at the time of Jack's murder. Once again this would not be any help in my ultimate goal to convince the police of the DeLoreon's role in Jack's death. Proof that a cover-up concerning Joseph's visit to Jack in Chicago would certainly raise suspicions about Jack's death the next day, but I would be unable to prove the nature of Joseph's visit or that a file was created or a blood sample was taken. Any information I acquired using my illegal methods must be followed up by gathering incriminating information via legal means if I had any hopes of bringing up murder charges against anyone.

Looking further into Joseph's assets I found all the real estate and bank accounts you would expect for his public charitable causes but I also found that Joseph owned the largest resort on the Bimini Islands. I assumed this was purely a profitable venture because I could find no evidence that he actually frequented or visited this resort on any regular basis even though it was fairly close to his home on Cat Cay Island. I tried my best to find photographs of Joseph to acquire proof that it was Joseph who visited Jack prior to his death. I could find numerous references to Joseph and the DeLoreon Foundation in newspapers in both the Bahamas and the United States, but no photos. His appearance proved to be even more elusive than his history and background. I could find no educational information on him, no birth records, no marriage license, no voting registrations, no driver's license, and in fact, no certifiable record of any kind bearing Joseph's name. Joseph was a ghost in a world of virtually unlimited electronic information gathering via the internet. It was getting more difficult to prove the man actually existed that it would be to prove he was involved in a murder. But then I came across something of interest. I was performing a scan of all Bahamas newspaper articles I could find relating to the DeLoreons (few as they might be) and in one article from the Bahamas Journal I came across a reference to the now-defunct Gulf Express. It was evidently a Bahamas newspaper that went out of business back in the early 60's. Though the original newspapers files were long since gone, I was able to find an archive of some of their articles on a Florida real estate firm's website. While scanning through the grainy low resolution photos I came across one that I enlarged with my printer. It was a photo of the ground-breaking for the DeLoreon Shores resort on the Bimini Islands built in 1956.

Hand-scrawled on the bottom of the photo were the words, "Owner Joseph DeLoreon shown in the background conferring with architect

William Jones". The photo of the man was not real clear so I could not make an accurate guess upon his age, but it appeared that the man in the photo must be somewhere between 40 and 70 years in age. I took into consideration the quality of the photo and the aging effects the sun can have on those living their whole life in an environment such as the Bahamas, but even going with the low end of my age range guess this would still make Joseph over ninety years old today. Jack placed the gentleman's age that visited him somewhere in the mid sixties so it did not seem likely that it was Joseph himself that visited Jack. Perhaps this was actually Joseph's father John. Or perhaps it was Joseph in the picture and Joseph appeared so young today to Jack because of his intense interest in cosmetic surgery and cosmetics. Wealthy people become obsessed with their age and maybe that was another reason for Joseph's appearance at Jack's office. From the contrast of the others in the photo it appears Joseph's skin was darker than most. I considered the possibility of Hispanic descent considering his complexion and last name and jotted down some notes for further research into the background of the DeLoreon family. I pulled out my magnifying glass for a closer inspection of the photo. While the whole photo had a grainy texture that could be attributed to its age or a low resolution scan, it still was apparent that there were marks on Joseph's face that did not match the pattern of the grain. Jack mentioned scars all over the face of the gentleman that visited his office and if the faint marks I was looking at on this aged photo were in fact scars, then this also led me to believe it actually was Joseph that visited Jack last week. Trying to piece together a timeline for Joseph and his father John, I figured Joseph would have been born between 1910 and 1920 based on using the low age guess from the photo. I still had not come across any photos of his father John so I jotted another note down to try and find a photo of his father. I also could find nothing in regards to a Mrs. DeLoreon in my research which also hampered my ability to do a background check on Joseph and John. I had already performed a search for the name DeLoreon in obituary notices in every country in the Western Hemisphere I could think of without any luck. So I expanded my search to Spain and Portugal based on my Hispanic theory but still had no luck matching anything to John or a spouse. Feeling I was at a dead end I decided to repeat my internet search pattern, only this time including the name DeLoreon in the content of files, not just the title. I decided to do this on all the newspapers I was previously unsuccessful in finding the name in a title or headline. This would take significantly longer and took the better part of a day to perform this search. During one lengthy search on a little known search engine I got up to stretch my legs and refresh my cup of coffee. When I returned to my computer I found that I had a solitary match. It involved a police dispatch report in the Bahamas Journal for a Mr. Earl Vedder who it appears was shot and killed by a security guard for the DeLoreon Foundation. It alleged that Mr. Vedder was attempting to break into the DeLoreon mansion on North Cat Cay Island on March 19, 1984, and he had a confrontation with the Island's security guards that ended up in his death. I used another technique I learned from another CIA agent to access the Bahamas police department archives and found a short police report matching the dispatch report attributing the death to self-defense by one of Joseph's security guards protecting the mansion during an attempted burglary. Something wasn't quite right here. Why was there no newspaper article about this event other than an obscure dispatch report? Certainly this would be newsworthy for the Bahamas Journal since violent deaths were probably not a daily occurrence.

I spent the rest of the evening tracking down the name Earl Vedder. I eventually found a death record for an Earl Vedder from Miami, FL that matched the date of the police dispatch report for the Bahamas. While it appears Earl had no children he did have a surviving spouse named Jane. Assuming she did not change her name or remarry, I focused my search on the name Jane Vedder. I was able to find a Jane Vedder living in Miami and hoped that this was Earl's surviving wife. While this could easily prove to be a wild goose chase my available strings to pull at in an attempt to unravel this mystery were dwindling rapidly. I decided I should take the time to verify that this was Earl's wife and to try and talk with her. I found her number in the phone book and gave her a call. I decided not to give her the option of pretending not to be Earl's wife if I came out and asked her the question. Instead I decided to make the call as if I was already sure of whom it was I was talking to. I made my call again from my untraceable Go-Phone.

"Hello?" she answered.

"Hello, Jane Vedder?" I asked.

"Yes it is, who is this?" she asked.

"My name is David Slater." I answered. "I am investigating criminal activity involving the DeLoreon Foundation and I've come to the conclusion that your husband's death in 1984 might be a result of a cover-up associated with this criminal activity. I was wondering if you would be willing to listen to my theories."

I figured this would be a lot of information to absorb for someone unrelated to Earl to take in and there would simply be an immediate response that I had the wrong number. The fact that there was silence for a few seconds told me I had the correct Jane Vedder. I also figured she would be reluctant to share any information with me over the phone, so instead elected to initiate the communication by saying I had something to share with her in hopes of using her curiosity as a ground breaker.

She finally answered.

"What sort of criminal activity are we talking about Mr. Slater?" she answered.

Contact established. As remote of a possibility this was for a new lead, I felt compelled to ensure I didn't alienate her. Personal contact was probably the best course here.

"Let's just say that I believe your husband might have been murdered for learning something about the Foundation that they wished to be kept secret. There has been another death, and I believe the two are related. Information like this might better be discussed in person, would there be a chance I could stop by your place later this week to share what I have learned with you? I asked.

"Yes you can Mr. Slater." She responded, "But if there is information you are expecting to get from me, I shared everything I knew years ago with the police. I probably wouldn't be able to help you in your investigation."

"I understand that Mrs. Vedder, but I feel compelled to share my suspicions with you and don't believe a phone call is appropriate for this. I will give you a phone call later this week when I am in your neighborhood if that is acceptable?" I asked.

"Yes, but please give me a little notice before showing up." She responded.

I intentionally did not state to Jane that I was associated with any specific law enforcement agency to give myself the option to gauge what would be more appropriate when I arrived. I would need to have a few different cover stories available when I showed up at her door.

I knew my wife would be significantly concerned with yet another cross-country flight over this investigation so I approached her with my idea to take a few days off from my P.I. duties and book us both into a beachside resort in Miami for four days and three nights. I was upfront about planning to squeeze in a visit to Jane Vedder to put to rest one final question I had about the case but I downplayed it significantly more than I probably should have. I spent the rest of the evening in fruitless research hoping to find other leads to pursue while my wife packed the bags. The souring economy was doing wonders for my travel plans since I would never have been able to book next day flights to Florida this easy in the past. Marcy hoped to convince me to relax a bit on the beach while in Miami to take my mind off of Jack and I conceded that she might be right in an effort to appease her concerns and allow me to continue my investigation. I made no mention of Jack the next day while Marcy and I finished our trip preparations and headed to the airport. During the flight I made it a point to go over the vacationing aspects of our visit with Marcy and unless my visit to Jane Vedder produced new leads I actually planned to do a little relaxing with my wife on the beach. I packed my laptop in my carry-on bag and tucked all my notes I had jotted down about the DeLoreons into its side pocket. Though I knew it would irritate Marcy if she knew, I also packed my traveling bag of tricks into my checked bag. I didn't see the need for the majority of these things for my visit with Jane but I hated to be unexpectedly caught in a situation where I needed one of my devices when I was on an extended trip.

Chapter 6

EARL VEDDER

MARCY AND I CHECKED INTO a beach front hotel late that evening and had a pleasant dinner. As painful as it was I was able to put aside my obsession with Jack's death for a short period of time and put on a romantic demeanor for Marcy that first evening. Though it was close to midnight when we actually retired to our room it was still only 9pm back home in Los Angeles and my wife and I typically stayed up late watching Television together. We ordered a pay-per-view movie after we retired to our room. I got up early the next morning and called Jane to arrange a visit. I then kissed my wife good-bye and told her to sleep in. I promised that I would make my visit to Jane Vedder's house as short as possible.

On my drive to Jane's house I went over in my head the questions I planned to ask her. I also did some heavy mental laboring over trying to remember what the movie was I watched with my wife the previous night. It was apparent that my mind was monopolized by Jack's death and until I had some closure I would not be able to concentrate on anything but this investigation for awhile. Though I had a variety of cover stories in my head when I knocked on Jane's door I've always had a knack for quickly adjusting to the situation and for some reason, when Jane answered the door I decided that the honest approach was the best. I told Jane that I was the gentleman that had called her the previous evening and introduced myself with my real name. Jane appeared to be in her late 40s and quite ironically fit the plain Jane profile. Though we were face to face at this moment, Jane left the screen door closed, so I sensed a bit of apprehension on her part concerning my motives for asking questions about a case over two decades old. I then explained further that I believed my best friend had recently been murdered by someone in the DeLoreon Foundation and that I believed my friend's death was linked to the death of her husband. For a moment her face was emotionless and I believed I might have misjudged the situation, and then I slowly saw pity creep into her expression. I've used pity as a cover for my investigations in the past but this was the first time I used it genuinely. She said she was more than willing to answer my questions but due to the fact she had only been married to Earl for 2 years over 20 years ago she was not quite sure what information I could possibly obtain from her that would be useful.

"Jane, do you have any idea why Earl went to Joseph DeLoreon's home back in 1984?"

"Earl was obsessed." Jane exclaimed.

"Excuse me Mrs. Vedder? Obsessed with what?" I asked.

"Joseph DeLoreon!" She responded. "I explained all this to the police over 20 years ago Mr. Gaites. I'm not sure what additional information you might want to obtain from me?"

"I'm sorry Mrs. Vedder. While it is true that I am an ex-police investigator, I am from Los Angeles and I don't have access to the Florida police department's files. My investigation is more personal than criminal, and I was hoping to hear more of your personal perspective on what happened back in 1984 than what the police records might say."

In addition to the pity I first saw in her eyes I could now see scrutiny. She was evaluating my sincerity and I sensed something akin to fear in her expression. I dared not lower my eyes and after a few more seconds of her looking into them she opened the screen door.

"Won't you please come in and sit down Mr. Gaites. I have kept much of Earl's death to myself for many years and if you have any chance of offering me some closure on this I would be willing to discuss it. But I doubt I have any information that would assist you anymore than I was able to assist the police back in 1984."

Jane escorted me to her living room and motioned for me to take a seat in one of the chairs facing the large window adjacent to her back yard. Outside this window was a spectacular garden that contrasted greatly with the appearance of her house from the front. There were two chairs here turned slightly askew towards each other with a small end table in between them with coasters. I figured this was a common place for her to sit and chat with a visiting friend. I felt obliged to comment on how lovely her garden was as she walked to the other chair. She turned and thanked me for my comment, and then paused a second. She then asked me if I would care for a cup of coffee and I accepted even though I had already had my morning cup of coffee. I believed sharing a cup of coffee with Jane might be beneficial in establishing a more relaxed and informative interview with her. Jane returned with a tray with two cups of coffee, a decanter of cream and another one of sugar on it. I waited a second to observe that Jane drank her coffee black, and then responded in kind by picking up my cup and taking a sip.

"You mentioned that Earl was obsessed with Joseph DeLoreon Mrs. Vedder?"

"You may call me Jane, Mr. Gaites." she responded.

"Please call me Jordan." I quickly interjected.

"Earl worked for the Fortress Security Company here in Miami and he spent two weeks installing a security system for Joseph one month after we married. Upon his return home he just kept saying something wasn't quite right about Joseph's island and he spent countless hours trying to find out more information on Joseph. This obsession lasted for almost two years. Fortress Security ultimately let Earl go in February of 1984 after the DeLoreon Foundation contacted his company complaining of Earl's poking his nose into their affairs. Evidently they somehow became aware of Earl's obsession and told Fortress Security that Earl was asking too many questions that were unrelated to his job. Earl bought himself a ticket to the Bahamas in early March and I never saw him again. The Bahamas Police department contacted me to tell me he was shot and killed trying to break into Joseph's private residence at North Cat Cay Island."

"Do you have any idea what it was that Earl was talking about when he said something wasn't quite right?"

"I'm sorry Jordan but Earl was very tight-lipped about it. Our relationship went down the drains from the moment he returned from the Island the first time his company sent him there. He spent the next 18 months either holed up in the basement or traveling around the country to various places trying to satisfy his curiosity. He just kept telling me that he needed proof but would never elaborate on what he was trying to prove. I know it had something to do with Joseph and his father John but Earl was so paranoid he told me it was best for my safety that he didn't share what he suspected with me. I shared all this information with the police but they ultimately believed that Earl was delusional."

"Do you believe the police story that Earl was shot while breaking into Joseph's private mansion?" I asked

"To some extent. I do believe Earl went there to try and satisfy his curiosity, but Earl would never have taken a gun with him. I don't believe he was shot in self-defense. I believe he was killed because of some secret he uncovered."

"Did he have any information in the basement to indicate what it was he was obsessed with?"

Again I saw the glimmer of hesitation and fear in her eyes but she eventually answered anyways.

"Only some pictures, some nonsensical notes and some drawings that I discovered hidden years after Earl's death."

"Do you still have those pictures and notes Jane?"

"It's all still down in the basement in a metal box. On the off-chance Earl's paranoia was justifiable I didn't mention Earl's notes to anyone when I found them. I too became paranoid when a newspaper reporter came here asking about Earl's reason for going to DeLoreon's Island."

"A newspaper reporter came asking about Earl?"

"Yes. He said a scandal involving the DeLoreon Foundation would be front page stuff implying that he would get to the bottom of Earl's death. But it was obvious to me that he only wanted to know what information Earl had on the DeLoreon Foundation and that there would be no front page story. He kept hinting that he might be able to clear Earl's name if he could prove that Earl had something other than burglary on his mind when he broke into Joseph's house. I grew suspicious of him when he stated that Earl broke into Joseph's house rather than use those words that reporters typically use like 'allegedly'. You have to understand that at that point Earl's death was still under investigation and Earl had not been publicly accused of any wrongdoing. I became immediately suspicious when he kept using words like burglary. When I explained to him that Earl shared nothing with me and left nothing behind explaining why he went to the Island, the reporter lost interest and left. I've not shared anything Earl left behind with anyone for over 20 years out of fear Jordan. I don't believe that was a real reporter that came to my house and I believe Earl knew something that scared the DeLoreons into killing him."

"Why are you sharing this with me now if you truly feared for your life concerning this information?" I asked.

"Because I don't believe Joseph would send someone out here 20 years later to ask me the same questions they asked me back in 1984. If Earl knew something that got him killed back then, then the information might still be dangerous today, but I don't have any reason to believe you have been sent by the DeLoreons, and I don't believe I possess any knowledge that would be a threat to them. I've always felt a slight sense of security in knowing that whatever it was that Earl knew, he took it to the grave with him. There is nothing I have learned from Earl's notes that could incriminate the DeLoreons and I've kept this information bottled up for over 20 years now. I am finding a sense of relief in finally sharing this information with someone. I hope this conversation is something you will keep strictly between you and me Jordan."

Though what the 'reporter' told Jane could very well have been true, I, like her, suspected otherwise. I believed it to be one of Joseph's hired thugs trying to find out if Earl shared anything with Jane or left anything behind that could hurt the DeLoreon Foundation.

"I can assure you Jane that anything you share with me will be strictly confidential. I am only out to find out why my friend was killed. If I were to uncover anything related to Earl's death I would clear it with you before sharing this information with the police or anyone else and I would never reveal my source of that information."

This time instead of paranoia and fear in her eyes I could see intense relief. It was obvious that Jane had bottled this information up inside her for all these years and not shared it with anyone. Even if she only had some nonsensical notes and drawings to share it was still a burden that she has waited years to get off her shoulders. Jane continued to share her feelings.

"After the visit by both the police and the reporter I went through Earl's things at least a dozen times to see if I could make any sense of it. I debated whether there might be some information that the police could use to prove that Earl did not attempt to break into Joseph's home but my fear outweighed any remote possibility the they would see any connection that I couldn't see. To be honest with you Jordan I firmly believe Earl did intend to break into Joseph's house and nothing in Earl's notes could prove whether or not Earl was shot in self-defense. Therefore nothing I could share with the police back then that would have eased the pain I went through. I've kept the box hidden in the basement in case anything surfaced in the news about the Joseph DeLoreon that might be related to Earl's death later and frankly I've just forgotten about it. As the days and then years went by without anything surfacing I became convinced that whatever secret it was that Earl was trying to expose would stay in his grave with him. Keep in mind Jordan that Earl was so distant from me at the time of his death I figured the best thing I could do was to get on with my life and put it all behind me."

There was a quiet uncomfortable pause at this point as I tried to suppress my curiosity about what was in Earl's box. Just as I was about unable to contain myself and was about to ask if I could see the box, Jane stood up.

"Let me get Earl's box." She said and walked to her kitchen door.

Jane turned back to me at this point and motioned for me to come with her. I followed Jane down to the basement and though it looked like the basement might have been an office many years ago it was obviously just a place for storage now. Jane got on her hands and knees and crawled under the ducting coming out of her furnace. She reached up behind the ducting and I heard the scrapping of metal against stone as she pulled a metal box out that was wedged up between the ducting and the cement wall of the basement. She motioned me to return with her to the living room and it became apparent that the only reason she wanted me to come with her to the basement was to impress on me how strongly she felt about keeping the box hidden these many long years. Allowing me to see her hiding place for the box was a part of easing the burden she had kept all these years. I followed her back to the living room and sat back in the chair I sat in when I first arrived. Jane sat in her chair and placed the box in her lap. She made no attempt to hand me the box and sat silently for a moment. She was obviously in heavy thought and I thought it best not to break the silence. Eventually she spoke.

"I haven't shared this box with anyone Jordan." She reiterated. "The first few years out of fear. Though I was skeptical of Earl's paranoia while he was alive I became very unsettled by the reporter's visit and chose to never share this box with anyone. After I gave up trying to find any clues to Earl's death in the box I chose to hide it in the basement and forget it. It's been there ever since. I doubt seriously you will find any information of use to you in here Jordan. But if I share it with you I have two requests."

"By all means Jane. Whatever you wish. What are your requests?"

"First, no one must ever know where you got this information in case there is anything in here that threatens Joseph DeLoreon. I have lived peacefully all these years since Earl's death and would like to keep it that way."

"And your other request Jane?"

"If you are able to discover whatever secret it is that got Earl killed I would like to be the first to know and then you must immediately make that information public. I did not sleep well for over a year after Earl died. Not knowing why I had lost my first love was painful enough. But also not knowing if Joseph would send someone after me suspecting that I also knew something I wasn't supposed to know caused me to always be looking over my shoulder or glancing in the car's rear view mirror. If Joseph is still alive and has a secret that Earl was killed for, the only thing that would make me feel safe is if I knew his secret wasn't a secret anymore."

"I can assure you that I will honor both of your requests Jane."

"I'll leave you alone to look over his papers Jordan." Jane exclaimed as she excused herself to the kitchen.

I dusted off the top off the metal box. I reflected for a second before opening it about how long it had been closed, and about how this was the last testament of Earl, having died for trying to find out whatever secret it was that I was now pursuing. Slowly I lifted the lid. The first thing I came across was his notes of dates and locations. The dates ranged from the late 1800's until the final date of 1956. The only date I recognized was the latter date associated with the ground breaking for the resort hotel. Whatever mystery Earl was tracking here it did not appear to be a recent one. The next thing I came to was a folded up detailed schematic of a security system. It included the floor plan for a large complex. Upon examination of the nomenclature and names of some of the rooms it became apparent to me that this was the security system that Earl helped install on Joseph's private island. No doubt he used this information to assist him in his failed attempt to gain access to Joseph's residence. I then came to a collection of 5 photographs. Somehow Earl had also happened upon the photo I acquired through the internet. But his was not a scan and had much greater clarity than the one I obtained. You could definitely make out the scars on Joseph's face in this photograph. The next 3 photographs were also of Joseph, but appeared to be personal photos with no historical or newsworthy value. I failed to see any relevance to any mystery in any of these.

But then I came to the last photograph and I stared at it quite some time trying to fathom its significance. It was a photo of John DeLoreon, and Earl had scrawled the words August 1928 on the bottom. As I stared at the photo of John it occurred to me that Joseph was the spitting image of his father. But what made my hair stand on end was the fact that John also was severely disfigured with facial scars. At first one would suspect that this was a photo of Joseph and that it was evidence of his being ageless, but a more rational response would be to believe that both father and son had severe facial scars. What possible custom or ritual would cause both father and son to suffered such wounds? Could this be some sort of self-inflicted rite of passage for some secret sect or society? John appears to be in his mid-50s for this photo, and being that I placed Joseph as being born just a few years earlier, I wondered just how much younger John's wife must have been than himself considering how old John must have been when Joseph would have been born. Try as I might, I could find no record of a wife for either John or Joseph in my previous research.

Out of the corner of my eye I saw that Jane was leaning against the door jam to the kitchen watching me intently.

"Did John ever show you these pictures Jane?"

"He kept them to himself. I never really saw them up close until a couple of years after his death. But I do remember coming home one evening while he was pre-occupied with them at our dining room table and I caught a glimpse of them before he covered them up."

"He didn't make any comments to you about the scars on both John and Joseph's faces?"

"He didn't make any comments to me about anything, yet I did hear him mutter to himself a few times about how could Joseph possibly be that old. It seems he was more concerned with Joseph's age than his appearance."

I compared the two photos again, and once again noticed the uncanny resemblance between the Joseph and John. Could it be Earl erroneously labeled another picture of Joseph as John? But if so, he would have to be wrong about the date also. Joseph couldn't have been more than a child in 1928.

Whatever secret these two possessed, Earl had given his life in pursuit of it. And now it appears the answers are hidden somewhere within the DeLoreon estate on North Cat Cay Island. Looking again at the security schematics for the DeLoreon mansion it became obvious to me that this was not just a security system to protect against burglary or trespassers. The nomenclature showed elaborate humidity and temperature controls and internal security which seemed designed to limit access to certain rooms even by people already inside the mansion. Evidently there were rooms that were designed to keep even the staff from seeing. The schematics showed a video surveillance system that was not limited to the exterior of the mansion but also included internal hallways and some rooms. Joseph is housing some secret there that was worth killing Earl over and it might very well have a bearing on Jack's death as well. Try as I might to think of another lead to pursue, it was slowly becoming apparent that my only chance of unraveling this mystery was hinged on my being able to find out what secret Joseph kept on his island. I looked back up at Jane who was still leaning on the kitchen door jam with her coffee cup cradled between both her hands.

"Jane, what would be the chances of my taking a few of Earl's photos and notes with me to help me try and solve the riddle Earl was obsessed with?"

"Take it all Mr. Gaites. Maybe getting rid of the box will assist me in getting on with my life and forgetting about Earl. I believe I have gotten over the agony of not-knowing the reason behind Earl's death but if you feel you can possibly solve it, please take it all. Don't bother to contact me again unless you have a conclusion for this story. I am in no mood for more speculation concerning something I have spent the latter part of my life trying to forget."

I thanked Jane for her time, and assured her that I would eventually get back to her, but only once I had a definitive answer to all of Earl's and my questions regarding the DeLoreon Foundation. I shook Jane's hand as she led me to the front door. I set the mysterious metal box on the car seat next to me as I drove back to my hotel room.

CHAPTER 7

TOP-SECURITY

MARCY WAS STILL ASLEEP (JET-LAG) when I got back to our hotel room so I studied the security schematics for quite some time. I noticed that the majority of the safeguards installed were to protect the west wing. It appeared there were redundant power supplies and automatic power switching units associated with the video surveillance and motion detectors. But the temperature and humidity sensors and controls were only associated with the West Wing. Something in the West Wing required strict environmental controls. Evidently, even though Earl possessed intricate knowledge of the security for the mansion, he was obviously unable to penetrate the DeLoreon fortress. What hopes did I have to gain access using security system schematics more than 24 years old? I needed an angle Earl didn't have if I was to gain any more information.

I quickly set aside the metal box as Marcy started to awaken. We had a brunch in the hotel lobby and then walked on the beach for an hour. We had only booked the hotel for two days here and my original plan only called for a short interview with Jane and the rest of the time vacationing with my wife. But I now had new information to go over that couldn't wait until I returned home. I thought it best to extend our stay another two days and Marcy was easily convinced it was a good idea. At this point I had no idea how I would maintain a vacationing attitude for my wife for the next few agonizing days without going bonkers over my desire to pursue this mystery further.

My wife knew I brought back paperwork I acquired from Earl's house, but she wisely avoided discussing the matter. She chose to participate in my pretense of vacationing and get out of it what she could in terms of time together on the beach, by the pool, at dinner and whatever other therapy she chose me to attend to try and distract me. Over the next 48 hours of quality family time I was able to steal a few momentary hours on my laptop. After reviewing my previously acquired financial information for the DeLoreons I was able to ascertain that the security systems at Joseph's mansion had been updated twice since Earl's death. The most recent security system update was eight months ago. I only knew this because of large payments made to Fortress Security, but had no idea what new and innovation security was added since Earl had installed the system over two decades earlier. A closer look at the financial transactions indicated that a Mr. James Dewey was the Foundation's representative that dealt with Fortress Security in Florida and he was the person signing all the checks for all the business transactions. I jotted down all the information I could uncover concerning these transactions and I believed I had come up with the angle I needed to gain access to Joseph's island. But I would need help. I made a few phone calls and set up an appointment with a graphical design studio a few blocks from our hotel. I excused myself from an afternoon massage appointment with my wife to go shopping, and while I understood my wife was not so naïve as to believe that shopping was my sole purpose, I still felt it was important to bring some token of sincerity back with me after my outing. Getting a bouquet of roses in addition to a little lingerie item for her might make up for missing the massage date. I was fortunate enough to hook up with their best graphical designer when I showed up for my appointment at Graphic's Express.

"I need a little assistance with you concerning my security designs. I am working on some potential security updates I need your assistance with, but I required that you not inquire as to the location of this system and keep our work strictly private." I informed their designer.

"Not a problem. I'm your man." He responded.

I unrolled Earl's security schematics on the designer's drawing board.

"First of all I would like a few cleaned up copies of this. For starters I want one copy with just the floor plan. Remove all the component details. Secondly, I would like a floor plan to include a new wing that I have sketched here." I said as I unfolded a sketch I had made of the current floor plan with an addition wing added next to the west wing. "I have a business appointment in two days with the client, can you complete this by tomorrow evening?"

"Sure, this is simple. Rush orders are no problem here if you have the money." He responded.

"That I do." I exclaimed.

I presented a few additional items I needed printed and left a deposit.

I stopped at two more specialty shops to acquire a few more props for my next masquerade. That done I returned to Marcy for another day of fun in the sun. The next evening I returned to Graphic's Express and picked up my various print jobs I had given them.

The next morning would be our last full day in Miami and I unfortunately had to break the news to Marcy that I again would be working on Jack's murder case for a few hours. As obsessed as I was, Marcy felt that my mixture of fun and work was sufficient to maintain my sanity and did not object to my next outing.

Fortress Security was on the other side of Miami and it took me about 30 minutes to get there in afternoon traffic. For my strategy this time I felt the need to show up unexpected. The entrance to the security office was designed to look like a bank vault. Fortress Security had the reputation of being the Rolex of security installation companies. I stepped up to the receptionist's desk and introduced myself.

"Hello. I'm Michael Jenkins and I'm here to have a word with your manager Charles Morgan."

"Let me see if he is in." the receptionist responded. "Can I let him know what it would be in regards to Mr. Jenkins?"

"Certainly. I am interested in upgrading our current Fortress security system and I would prefer to deal with Mr. Morgan directly."

The receptionist depressed the button on her office intercom.

"Mr. Morgan. There is a Mr. Jenkins here who would like to discuss some security system upgrades with you. Are you available?"

"Yes Nancy. I have a few minutes. Send him in."

"Right this way Mr. Jenkins. I will show you to Mr. Morgan's office."

As a Private Investigator it was in my nature to examine my surroundings. Assuming that my task at hand might involve circumventing many of the security features that were prominently displayed I glanced at all the various devices hanging in the hallway as we approached Mr. Morgan's office. I was here to have a quick conversation with Charles Morgan and then get on my way and arouse as little suspicion as possible. So it was a balancing act between how much attention I could risk examining the surroundings. Keeping my attention on the subject at hand, as hard as it might be, was necessary to keep from arousing suspicion of the real intention of my visit. Mr. Morgan was seated at a very large cherry wood desk as we entered his office. It was time for my quick cover story.

"Good afternoon Mr. Morgan. My name is Michael Jenkins. I am so sorry for the unscheduled visit but James Dewey asked me if I could stop by and fire a few quick questions your way. We are building a new wing out at the DeLoreon place and even though it's still in the design stage, I was hoping you could take a cursory look at our plans to let us know if there should be anything architecturally we might want to consider for it to be compatible with your latest security systems. I would hate to get our plans finalized only to have you look them over later and have you tell us we need to make major changes to make it compatible with your security system."

Charles Morgan was obviously taken aback a bit.

"I'm a little unprepared for your visit Mr. Jenkins. Should we perhaps set up an appointment for a thorough examination of your security needs?"

"Oh yes Charles. May I call you Charles?" I asked. "I fully plan to set a whole afternoon aside for this in the next couple of weeks, but James is mostly curious about any new innovations you might have for us and this is just an informal visit to give you a heads up and get us started on any major design changes you might suggest based on new security technology we are unaware of. While we understand you have installed your top of the line system in our west wing we would like the security for this new wing to be even more state-of-the-art. We have already incorporated into our new design all the same features you put in the old wing. We wouldn't be needing any of the elaborate temperature or humidity controls for the new wing but we were hoping you have something new we can use for this addition that would provide even more added security. You know Joseph is a fanatic about security on the island. Do you mind if I take a minute to show you what we are tentatively planning?"

At this point I have still not requested anything specific from Charles and am still working on establishing the credibility of my cover so while I still saw hesitation on his face I did not see any suspicion yet. Now for the bread and butter of my presentation. I must quickly convince Mr. Morgan I am who I say I am and put his mind at ease. I unrolled my newly printed blue prints on his desk and immediately pointed to the new addition I had the graphic artist add. My hopes was to distract Charles from scrutinizing the existing floor plans too much in case there were additions to the structure added since 1984 that were not present on my plans.

"This is where we plan to add a wing Charles." My drawing was only the basic floor plan since I had Graphics Express remove the security portions of the drawing. I had no idea how accurate the security portion of Earl's drawing was after so many years. I let my hand wander over to where the security system's independent power supply was located on the 24 year old schematics I obtained from Jane. I extended my index finger and leaned on the map such that if the power system was still there it would show my knowledge of the location, but if the power system had moved in the last 24 years, I wanted it to appear that I might just be leaning on the drawing with my finger extended. Before ever arriving at Fortress Security I had already rehearsed a few leading questions designed to elicit information from Charles. My hopes were that Charles would reveal vital information based on my vague generic questions. Next came the first of my leading questions.

"We would like the new security sensors to use the existing power system. So if there are any major changes you think we should consider in terms of floor plans or wall location, you might be able to make some suggestions when I set up an appointment next month. All the walls of the addition will be heavily reinforced, so we will have to work out with you the details about routing of the power and sensors and such, but that can wait until a lengthy meeting later. All I would ask at this time is if you foresee any major conflicts with this new floor plan with the existing system that we might be able to work through before we sit down with you to work out our new security measures."

Mr. Morgan studied the prints for a full minute and I was now becoming increasingly agitated. I could feel a bead of sweat start to form on my brow as I waited for my charade to be exposed. My whole strategy was based on his having enough knowledge of the security system to buy my cover story, yet not enough knowledge to be able to answer my questions based on my plans alone.

Then Charles stood up straight, looked at me, and after a slight pause:

"Wait right here Mr. Jenkins."

He left, and I was left alone in his office. I didn't know if he was leaving to call the police, make a phone call to the DeLoreon Foundation or just to get himself a cup of coffee. During this uncomfortable absence I now had the opportunity to examine the various security devices displayed in his office. In this case, examining these devices was probably good for my cover of wanting to know about the latest and greatest security devices. I also wandered the office to try and cover up my anxiety over Charles leaving me alone in case anyone was watching my actions via security cameras. After all, this was a security company, and it was not unreasonable to believe there would be security monitors in the company's president's office.

Charles returned in just over two minutes with a cardboard tube in his hands. He unrolled his own set of blueprints, and, as I hoped, it was the current security system for the DeLoreon's mansion. I was somewhat relieved to notice that the power system was still in the same location on Charles' drawing as where I was pointing when I addressed the issue of power. I believed my pointing to the location of the power supply even though it was not displayed on my drawing had the effect I had planned in supporting my identity. Charles was truly convinced I was who I was masquerading to be. I now had two tasks left at hand. First, I needed to gleam another tidbit or two about the system from Charles without drawing suspicion of my ignorance of the current system. Second, I needed to keep Charles talking long enough for me to scrutinize the drawing he was showing me without giving off the appearance of never having seen this drawing before. I pulled out my special set of reading glasses, the ones with a miniature digital camera built into the frames and snapped off a shot or two as I leaned over while adjusting them on my ears. My scrutiny was not needed for memory since I would have photos to scrutinize later. My looking at the drawing was more so to see if I have any new spontaneous questions based on something I might see that differed from Earl's drawing. In this case I might be able to elicit even more useful information than what I had originally planned.

Pointing at the print with my left hand to get Charles to look at the print I adjusted my glasses with my right hand to take my photos. While the photos would prove invaluable I still needed to quiz Charles to gather information. I also coordinated the ever so quiet click of the camera with my voice.

"We plan to get the power and sensor lines to the new wing via this wall over here. Do you foresee any issues with this such that we might need to consider major changes to our floor design as shown on my print?"

This was idle chit-chat here for the most part, and while lending an ear to Charles' response I noticed his drawing displayed several security camera locations not reflected in the drawing I obtained from Earl's wife Jane. If I were to ask any questions about his drawing, I must do so in the context of discussing with him our plans for the future wing. Any questions I might come up with after examining my photos of Charles' updated drawing later would remain unanswered. I must examine the drawing quickly and develop questions quickly. I saved some of my planned canned questions to fill in the gaps between questions I might have about his new drawing. My hopes were that Charles would feed me information not revealed in the drawings. His response did exactly that.

"We can install our conduits in this wall just as we have for the west wing. It would require a short run down this existing wall over here to reach the wing and we would have to tear into the existing reinforced concrete wall here (pointing) to add the new conduits. But I see nothing that would require you to deviate from your current floor plan. You should still sit down with me and my engineer for a more lengthy planning meeting later."

"Yes. I will talk with your receptionist about scheduling that meeting after we complete our planning meeting next week with our architect." I responded.

Here I learned that the conduit housing the security system wires was embedded in reinforced concrete and therefore probably not accessible between connection locations should I get to that point. I would have to gain access to the power room itself if I had any chance of disabling security cameras. I also made a mental note that even though there were numerous cameras in the corridors throughout the building, there didn't appear to be any evidence of cameras in the west wing itself. While I believed what was in the room must be of great value it appeared that DeLoreon was also intent on keeping the contents a secret from his own security force. This might work to my advantage. Before arriving at Fortress I considered a plan to disable the entire system at the main power supply since no back-up system was displayed on my old prints. I needed some clue as to whether this was feasible. The wording of my questions were such that they should not reveal my ignorance about certain aspects of the security system yet elicit a response that provides more information than what was contained in my question.

"Is the existing power supply adequate to support the new alarms, sensors and cameras for the new wing, or will we need to upgrade that as well?"

"The existing system should be adequate as long as you plan the same type safeguards as for your existing wing. However, the back-up system and generator down in your grotto was not designed for continuous operation with an added load such as this. Your back-up power supply will have to be upgraded."

More bad news. Now I not only know he has a back-up system, but I have no idea where it is located since there is no grotto displayed anywhere on my floor plans. I wonder if this is something that was added since Earl's assault attempt or simply something left out of the floor plans for the estate itself. Time for another leading question.

"We are happy with the existing safeguards you have installed for us in the west wing, but if you have any suggestions for improvements or upgrades we might install in our new wing I'm sure Joseph would consider anything you might recommend for added security. He is always fascinated by the latest and greatest technical advances."

"Well, it's been awhile since we installed your system and while your fingerprint scanning modules are still considered adequate for most security applications, they can be fooled. What James and Joseph might want to consider upgrading to is retinal scanners. Fooling a retinal scanner is near impossible and if you truly wish to stay state-of-the-art on your security system you might want to consider this. An added feature we can offer with these scanners in an integral battery back-up in the module itself. With your current fingerprint scanners, if you were to have a devastating earthquake or disaster disabling both your primary and backup power systems you could find yourself locked inside. While this still provides security it could pose a safety hazard. These internal batteries would maintain the operability of those retinal scanners for up to 24hrs after a power interruption allowing you to either enter or exit even with both your power supplies out of commission. You might want to consider upgrading your existing fingerprint scanners to stand-alone power systems also."

This was more bad news. I was hoping for a keypad entry system or some sort of lock I could disable or pick to get into the west wing. A fingerprint sensor would pose an obstacle I hadn't planned on. Charles also revealed that on a loss of power the fingerprint scanning locks failed shut such that disabling both the primary and backup power systems would not give me access to the west wing. I had exhausted my canned questions and could not come up with any new questions quickly so I figured it was time to gracefully exit rather than arouse suspicions by studying a drawing I should already be familiar with too intently. I stood up straight and faced Charles.

"I feel confident Joseph and James will both be interested in your retinal scanner upgrade. I will present that to them at our next planning meeting and work out a schedule for sitting down with you to design our new wing's security system. Thank you so much for taking time out to talk with me Charles. I look forward to working with you on this in the near future. There is also one last favor you could do for me."

"What might that be Mr. Jenkins?"

"We were running some security drills on our staff and one of our guards monitoring the system remarked that he saw fluctuations in the camera signals. Possibly some sort of electrical interference or water damage grounding our signal?" I asked.

"Yes, that could be a possibility." He responded.

"Could you possibly schedule a routine maintenance check of our system in the near future? Basically just run our system through your standard checks to make sure it's functioning properly?" I asked.

"Talk with Nancy before you leave and she can set that up for you. She has our maintenance technician schedule and can let you know when our openings are?" he responded.

"Thank you again Charles. I will get in contact with you in the coming weeks to set up a more formal visit to arrange for the design of our new wing's security system and upgrades for our existing system in the west wing."

I shook Charles' hand, gave him a friendly nod and excused myself from his office. I stopped at Nancy's desk and told her that Charles thought it was a good idea to have a routine check of the DeLoreon security system and asked if she could find a time available as soon as possible. Nancy checked her appointment book to look for an opening.

"We have an extra technician available all day Thursday. Would sometime Thursday be acceptable Mr. Jenkins?" she asked

"That would be perfect Nancy."

"Would time would you like him to be there?"

"Early afternoon. We have some visitors coming during the morning and I would prefer the system remain active until they leave. So just in case your serviceman needs to power down the system it would be better if that takes place after our visitors leave."

"What time would you prefer?" Nancy asked.

"How about 1 p.m.?" I responded.

"1 p.m. it is. Let me write that down here in my calendar right now."

"You have our number in your rolodex don't you Nancy?" I asked.

"Yes I do Mr. Jenkins." She responded.

"Could you call our office then and inform them that Mr. Morgan would like to schedule a routine check of our system? Could you also tell me where your rest room is?"

Nancy was very cooperative and as hoped, the visitor bathroom was within earshot of Nancy's desk. I listened at the doorway to Nancy's phone call. I was taking a chance here that Nancy would not bring up my name in her phone call, but I could not think of any manner in which I could ask her to not mention my name without arousing suspicion. But Nancy did just as I asked, and told whoever was at the other end of the phone that Charles Morgan at Fortress Security would like to set up a routine check of their system. From this end of the conversation it went flawless. It appeared they wanted the exact time to expect their technician and she set it up for him arriving by boat at their docks at 1 p.m. After she completed her phone call I flushed the toilet and washed my hands to complete the charade and then returned to Nancy.

"Okay Mr. Jenkins. We are all set up for your maintenance visit at 1 p.m."

I pretended to be in deep thought and wrinkled my brow.

"Oh wait Nancy. I forgot about a V.I.P. visit we are having for lunch. You know Nancy, I'm thinking that 1 p.m. does not give us enough time to wrap-up with our visitor. Could you change that visit to 3 p.m. instead?" (Pointing at her calendar in front of her)

"Sure thing Mr. Jenkins." I watched as she erased the time of the appointment on her calendar and changed it to 3 p.m.

I quickly stepped a couple of feet away from her desk and pretended to make a cell phone call to the island security manager explaining that we were pushing the maintenance visit back two hours to 3 p.m. and also asked the security manager to set up an appointment between myself and James Dewey to discuss my visit with Fortress Security. I hung up the phone and then glanced back at Nancy.

"So we're all set for 3 p.m. this Friday Nancy?"

"Yes Sir." she responded and made no hint at any attempt to make another phone call based on the call she heard me make.

Assuming that no contact would take place between the island and Fortress Security between now and Thursday, island security would be expecting a technician at 1 p.m., while Fortress Security would not actually be sending a technician until 3 p.m. This would give me two hours to pose as a Fortress Security technician and do what I needed to do.

As I exited the building I immediately pulled out my back pocket notepad and jotted down a number while it was still fresh in my memory. I assumed it was a model number for modules on Charles' drawing located at both the entrances to the west wing. I could only hope this was the model number for the fingerprint sensors required to gain access. I was worried that the detail of my spy camera might not be sufficient to read the model numbers.

I returned to my wife with not one, but three meaningless souvenirs from Miami. This was a futile attempt to appease Marcy for the news that I would not be accompanying her on the flight home in the morning. I simply told her I had a few more leads to follow up on and that I would catch a flight home in two days (Thursday evening). This would give me the rest of Wednesday and Thursday morning to prepare for my visit to North Cat Cay Island.

CHAPTER 8

ASSAULT PREPARATIONS

ISLAND ACCESS – I FOUND out that while Joseph DeLoreon possessed a helo-pad on his island, the primary means of access was via boat. Nancy had mentioned the technician arriving by boat, so I researched boat rentals in the area. I found a rental boat from the nearby resort island of Bimini and made a reservation for one of their ski boats along with a reservation for a night's stay at their resort hotel. My cover for anyone I encountered prior to going to North Cat Cay would be that of the casual tourist. I printed out a large version of the Fortress Security logo, and took it down to Kinkos where I was able to produce various professional looking color logos on peel and stick vinyl for my toolbox, binder and a few other items. I also was able to get a local embroidery company to produce an authentic Fortress Security logo above the pocket of a polo shirt with matching khaki pants. They should be expecting a technician from Fortress Security at 1 p.m. on Thursday and I planned to produce one for them with as many props as I could to support my role. I visited a local security company under the pretense of being interested a new security system, but explained that I wanted a system that would last for decades, and asked to see what types of maintenance checks and inspections they would do to ensure its longevity. They obliged by showing me their check off sheets and maintenance logs they used to verify the proper operation of their systems. My spectacle Spycam photos of these forms greatly assisted me in preparing the fake paperwork I would need to take with me to North Cat Cay. I also pilfered a blank piece of paper with Fortress Security's letterhead on it when Nancy was busy with her calendar planning my visit. This came in handy for creating much of my fake paperwork. I combined the security information from the 24 year old drawing with what I could remember from my visit to Fortress to prepare new blueprints to bring along. I also prepared a hard plastic Fortress Security Identification badge to hang from my lapel. Company letterheads and forms are one of the easiest things to fabricate in our present day age of an over abundant number of graphics software programs designed to perform that purpose. So there was no reason not to include various forms and letters in my masquerade collection. You can never have too many props. It's amazing just how much software there is that is designed for legitimate purposes that can be used to deceive if placed in the wrong (or in my case, right) hands.

FINGERPRINT SCANNER – I searched the internet for the model number I had jotted down when I left the Fortress office. It seemed there was a DVD player and a 1960's record player in addition to a fingerprint access scanner with that model number. The fingerprint scanner was available at several security service companies across the country. I could have acquired one from Fortress but elected to stop by their local competitor here in Miami instead. I purchased one and played with it all afternoon in my hotel room. I employed numerous fingerprint lifting techniques I learned from my past experience on the police force and in the CIA. But I had limited luck applying the extracted print in a manner to get the sensor to accept the lifted print as being an actual finger. While I had hoped that a fingerprint left on glass would be the easiest to use, I was only successful about half the time with transferring it to a usable form for the scanner. Eventually I found that I had better luck lifting a print off of highly polished stainless steel coated with a very thin layer of a special silicone gel I had luckily packed in my bag of tricks. But this was still not 100% successful and I had several other obstacles I needed to overcome if I was going to succeed in getting access to the west wing. First I must find someone who has access to the wing via the fingerprint pad. Second I must get this person to leave their fingerprint on something I can use. Third I would have to hope I used the correct finger encoded into their access files. I would just have to assume it would be their right index finger.

ESCORTS – I couldn't downplay the possibility that even though I am to be considered the expert on their security system, they still might be concerned with keeping an eye on me while I worked. I was preparing an elaborate set of devices to possibly give me the excuse to stray away from my escort. The most promising one was the fake test gear I would prepare that would require a second technician to monitor an indication while I performed tests in another location. I brought along my Motorolas which would allow us to stay in contact and while it would appear that lights and a meter on the test equipment were operating based on my manipulation of wires and connections, in reality I would have a wireless remote control located in my pocket that activated the indications. This would give the person at the other end the impression I was still manipulating wires where he left me when in fact I would simply be pressing buttons on my remote and talking to him on the Motorola while roving the complex. I had a few other tricks up my sleeve should this one not serve the purpose.

SECURITY CAMERAS – While I assumed the cameras would be hooked up to a recording device, a recording of my visit did not concern me. I planned to be in and out in under an hour. It was continual live monitoring of the system that was my concern. There was only one camera I would need to pass to get from the power supply room to the west wing according to my blueprints. I stocked my toolbox with a few devices to help if this was the case. The easiest plan would simply be to convince them I must disable the cameras for my checks. But I must have a back-up plan if this was unacceptable to them. I also prepared a very small 5-sec loop recording device I would attempt to place in line with the camera I would need to pass to access the room. I would simply record the existing camera signal for 5 seconds and then put it on a continuous loop playback. The device was disguised to look like a video signal tester if I was being monitored while installing it. If I could get by that one camera, once I was in the west wing I would be invisible to the guards. That is, provided I was also able to disable the various motion sensors installed. I arrived in Miami late Wednesday night, and acquired a charter boat to the Bimini resort very early Thurday morning.

CHAPTER 9

ASSAULT NORTH CAT CAY ISLAND

I ARRIVED ON BIMINI ISLAND at 8 a.m. Thursday morning. My room was not yet prepared for check-in but they did allow me to leave my one clothing bag in the room while the maids were attending to it. The remainder of my items I planned to take with me on a rental boat to North Cat Cay. I figured it might draw a little too much attention changing into my Fortress Security uniform prior to leaving the resort hotel so I planned on doing that en route. I killed a couple of hours surveying Bimini island's recreational facilities (owned by the DeLoreon Foundation) and renting a 15 foot power boat. I then placed a phone call to Nancy at Fortress Security to try and gauge if my cover had been blown.

"Nancy, Michael Jenkins here from North Cat Cay Island. Our schedule here today is pretty hectic, so I just wanted to double-check that we still a go for our 3 p.m. check of our security system?"

"Yes sir Mr. Jenkins. Our technician will be there promptly at 3 p.m." she replied.

"Thanks again Nancy. I'll be seeing you in a few weeks then when I come back into your office."

It was a 30 min trip to North Cat Cay Island. I stopped just out of visual range of North Cat Cay to change into my uniform. I noticed I was still going to arrive about 10 minutes early for my appointment so I utilized this extra time to look over my props, forms and equipment while bobbing around in the waves. I bobbed for an additional 5 minutes after my preparations so as not to arrive too soon at the island. I pulled up to the island's dock promptly at 1 p.m.

As I approached I didn't see anyone waiting there to meet me and I started to get a little on edge thinking of Earl's failed attempt to access this island. But as I got closer I then saw a guard exit a solitary phone booth type enclosure at the head of the dock. He assisted me in tying off the boat and made no communication at all during that process. I took this as a sign they were expecting me. He motioned me to follow him and we made our way to his cubical. It was about a 4ft by 4ft wooden booth, had a single wooden bar stool and a drop-down desktop. I would think with the wealth of the DeLoreon Foundation that they could afford something a little more comfortable. But then I reasoned that the intent was that the guard not be so comfortable so as to keep him awake in what appeared to be a very boring job. The guard entered the booth and picked up a phone and made a call.

"Mr. Dewey. Fortress Security has arrived." He spoke into the phone. There was a pause as he listened to James Dewey's response. As he listened he turned and looked at me. He didn't look me in the face but instead was examining my uniform and general appearance to gauge whether I looked like a maintenance technician.

At this point I was feeling pretty confident that the 1 p.m. appointment still existed and that no communication had taken place since Nancy scheduled the visit. The guard talked briefly with James Dewey and I waited patiently to see what James' response was.

"Ok Mr. Dewey, I will tell him." He hung up the phone.

"Mr. Dewey will be down shortly to talk with you." he exclaimed and then turned to his desk. I was a little uneasy about the head of security himself coming down to talk with me. I had already planned a situation requiring me to talk with Mr. Dewey after my arrival so that I could acquire his fingerprint, so this might be a blessing in disguise. On the guard's desk was a ledger he started to write in. It appeared to be a log of whatever transpired on his watch. The only other items on his desk were a calendar, a coffee cup and an intercom. He motioned me to his opened ledger. He pointed at an entry filled out for Fortress Security and instructed me to print and sign my name. While I did this, he depressed the intercom button and in a short gruff manner informed the person at the other end "Fortress Security is here. One technician." I can only assume he was informing someone else other than James Dewey of my arrival. After filling out the ledger, the guard asked for identification and seemed satisfied with both the Florida Driver's License and Fortress Security ID I presented. He also required me to open my toolbox and looked over each device though I had the feeling he had no concept as to what purpose each device in my toolbox held. Once satisfied I wasn't bringing any weapons with me the guard handed me an island security badge. He advised me to attach it to my shirt pocket and cautioned me that I must wear it for the entire duration of my visit to the island.

"Your escort will be here shortly." He informed me.

I stepped away from the guard's enclosure and surveyed my surroundings. With my back to the guard, I unclipped my security badge and examined it. The bulge in the molded plastic led me to believe that each badge assigned to visitors contained a tracking device allowing their security to keep tabs on their visitor location at all times. I reattached the badge and then examined what I could see of the island. There were several sets of stair landings alternating left and right built into the side of the cliff separating the docks from the DeLoreon mansion about 75 feet above. I did not look forward to this climb. I had a 20 pound toolbox I would need to carry up those stairs. Up at the top of the stairs I could see an armed guard looking down at us, but he made no indication that he was coming down to greet me or help me with my toolbox. Just then the side of the cliff to the left of the stairs opened up. It was obviously a service elevator that had been cleverly disguised to match the cliffs. My feet and aching back welcomed the sight of this elevator.

The gentleman that exited the elevator introduced himself to me as James Dewey, none other than the security manager I had namedropped during my visit to Fortress Security. I introduced myself as Paul Kamp and said I was here to perform a routine maintenance check on their security systems.

"Yes, we know about your visit Mr. Kamp. Did you have engine trouble Mr. Kamp?" James asked.

"Excuse me sir?" I responded.

"We noticed on our radar you seemed to be stranded out there for almost 10 minutes. We were about to dispatch a boat to check to see if you were in trouble."

I made an attempt to suppress my slight panic and had to come up with an answer quickly.

"Oh no sir. I over estimated the time it would take to get to your island, and Charles Morgan cautioned me about being prompt on my arrival. I didn't want to disrupt any schedule you might have here by arriving early."

After a slight hesitation on his part he seemed satisfied with this answer. He then motioned me to follow him into the elevator. I stopped at the recessed door entrance to examine the fake foliage concealing the elevator entrance. While doing this I turned slightly to allow my body to block his view of my left hand removing my flashlight from my hip holster.

"My time is valuable Mr. Kamp, we need to get a move on and complete your inspection so you can be on your way." He cautioned me.

"I'm sorry Mr. Dewey. It's just that this is my first time to the island, and I am fascinated. I've never seen an elevator so cleverly hidden inside a cliff like this"

"It's not 'hidden' Mr. Kamp! Joseph prefers to keep the outer edges of the island as close to natural as possible. This is simply his home and he prefers it to be as private, secure and comfortable. The elevator design is for aesthetics and not security."

I continued to stare at the foliage above the door as I stepped into the elevator to conceal my intentional trip on the door jam as I entered. My toolbox flew to the right, and my flashlight slid to the left between James' feet just as I aimed. I apologized for being so clumsy as I gathered myself up. I brushed off my knees and grabbed my toolbox to my right as James bent over and picked up my flashlight to return to me. I placed the flashlight back in my belt pouch being careful to not touch the flashlight anywhere near where I noticed his right index finger was touching it. The highly polished surface of the flashlight had the light silicon coating that proved to be the best fingerprint transferring surface.

After the short quiet elevator trip up, the door opened to another guard at the top of the cliff. James introduced this guard to me simply as "George" and informed me that George would be my escort for my visit. James then left to continue whatever he was doing before I arrived. I introduced myself to George hoping to strike up an informal acquaintance. But George would have none of that and simply motioned me to follow him. After we entered the mansion itself George asked me where I would like to start. I informed him I would definitely like to start in the power supply room but would also like to inspect the sensors in the west wing. George informed me:

"No one enters the west wing other than Joseph or James."

He explained that my maintenance inspection would have to be limited to components outside the west wing. This was both good and bad news. The bad news was that I would not be able to access the west wing at all for my checks. This also presented the obstacle to my Escort separation plan involving my being at the sensors while the guard communicates with me from the power room.

But the good news was that James Dewey had access to the west wing and I had James' fingerprints on my chrome flashlight as planned. George's statement also reaffirmed my belief that no security personnel would be present in the west wing if I was able to gain access.

George escorted me to the power supply room and unlocked the door via a fingerprint scanner to let me in. The room had transformers and isolation panels mounted to the right wall. The left wall supported a horizontal apron section of controls and a vertical panel that housed twelve monitors for security cameras located throughout the complex. Various alarm modules were mounted to the left and to the right of the monitors and there were access panels below the three apron sections. The room was very small which was good in that it would be very cramped if George planned to stay in the room with me while I performed my inspection. On the off chance he did hang out with me I figured I would start out by laying prone to access the floor panels. This would prove to be the most cramped position and it might be an incentive for him to leave.

"Am I going to be in your way while I'm inside these access panels?" I said while pointing to the floor panels.

"Not at all." He responded. "This room is not manned. We watch the monitors from the security room on the other side of the complex. I will leave you alone here to complete your work. You will need to get permission prior to disabling any of our monitors or sensors."

"The majority of my checks can be done here with the system energized.' I informed him.

George had provided me with both good and bad news. Another room, more guards, and more monitors

"How will I contact you when I am ready to de-energize some systems?" I asked.

"Just open the door and remain here. Don't make any attempts to leave unescorted, just open the door and I will be with you shortly." He answered.

"Thank you George. The tests I am performing first could take up to an hour but I will open the door and wait for you prior to checking anything outside this room."

I noticed the door had intrusion sensors mounted on the inside of the door and that was how George would know when I was ready to leave. He would also be able to view me on the camera located at the end of the hall between the power room and the west wing so he felt pretty secure in leaving me in the room alone. George closed the door behind him as he left. I now felt trapped. The good news is that the door sensors were designed to alert the guards when someone was trying to gain access to this room but easily manipulated from the inside to prevent alerting the guards that someone was exiting the room. Accessing the door sensors from the outside would be impossible, but disabling them from the inside was child's play. While it was within the scope of my inspection to kill power and go outside this power supply room, I could only do so under the direct supervision of George and that would not suit my plans. Killing power to the cameras so I could wander freely did not seem like an option at this point because of another room monitoring the signals. As I pondered my position, I examined the security system. I was quite familiar with these sort of systems. While the sensors and fingerprint scanning devices might be more sophisticated than what I normally encountered in my P.I. practice, it was still within the scope of my CIA espionage training. The power supplies, battery back-up and circuitry in this room were pretty standard. Nothing fancy required here. Just keep the system powered up. I was quickly able to verify Mr. Morgan's information that if I interrupted power to the fingerprint pads that the west wing would become inaccessible. There were schematics laminated to the door panels that confirmed that electrical solenoid operation was required to hold the spring loaded locks open for normal access. I must succeed in extracting James's fingerprint from my flashlight to operate the west wing door. And I still needed to get out of this room undetected and to the west wing. Closer examination of the power room door sensor confirmed my original surmise. It appeared that the only safeguard built into this device was the fact that you could not access it from outside the door. It was easily bypassed from the inside. I also found the intrusion alarm for the west wing was powered from this room and I bypassed that circuit so that the door could be opened without setting off an alarm or alerting any guards in the other monitoring room. The remaining circuitry was a little more elaborate than what I typically worked on but was not beyond my comprehension. The motion detection sensors had a loss of power alarm and also appeared to have power on indication lights. There were additional wires attached to the power available lights which I assumed sent the same indication to the other security room. I only needed to disable the motion detection in the hallway to the west wing and the west wing itself. I installed some jumpers to the keep the power available lights illuminated and the loss of power alarms energized prior to disabling the motions detectors. Roving security would not be necessary as long as security was able to monitor intrusion and motion detection from their security room. That and their continual video monitoring would hopefully keep me from running into any of them during my short movement to the West Wing.

Now to tackle the video surveillance issue. I examined the monitors on the apron section of the security panel. I was able to identify which one was for the hallway between the power supply room and the west wing because I saw George transverse it immediately as he left me alone to do my work. That and the convenient schematics on the panel doors had also confirmed this. Accessing the panel beneath the monitors I could see both an input and output signal to each monitor. This was very good news. The security camera feeds came through this power supply room before feeding the other security room George mentioned. I pulled as much slack as I could in the feeder line for the camera I must get by, and proceeded to slowly strip insulation away from the copper taking great care not to break the leads or short them out to each other. I hooked into the signal with alligator clips from my toolbox, and then hooked up their feed to my portable 5-sec video recorder. I fiddled with this for three or four minutes wasting valuable time before it dawned on me that the video signal was analog and not digital. I had just assumed their video surveillance was modernized, but it appears it hadn't been upgraded in several years and was still using an old analog signal. I was not prepared to deal with this and it appeared I was facing an insurmountable obstacle here not having any device to convert the analog signal to a recordable digital video signal. The west wing was only 30 yards away and I had no method to reach it without being observed by guards in another room on a video monitor.

As I pondered my problem I stared at the video feeds. It occurred to me that the #2 camera in my hallway had a video signal almost identical to that of the #8 camera in the north hallway. I quickly pulled out a double-throw switch from my toolbox and set about splicing the #2 feed to one side of the switch. I then spliced the #8 feed into the other side of the switch, and hooked up the switch output to the input to the #2 feed to the other security room. I watched closely as I cut the feed line from the #2 camera. The monitor continued to display the #2 camera through my switch since at this point all I did was bypass the wire I just cut. Now the test. I watched the monitor closely as I threw the switch to change the #2 feed to the #8 feed. There was a slight flicker of the monitor, but now the #2 display was identical to the number #8 display. Just prior to switching, I examined the 2 monitors for differences and I noticed a slight change in an electrical outlet location as I threw the switch. but other than that, the two hallways were identical. I flicked the switch back to #2, and there was a slight flicker again. I assumed if the guards in the other room were watching the monitors closely they might observe flicker, but they would just attribute it to the tests I was performing. I left the monitor on it's original feed while I took the next 10 minutes to extract James' fingerprint to a thin Mylar strip I then attached to the index finger of a tan colored latex glove.

I was ready. During the entire time I was in the room I observed absolutely no traffic on any of the security cameras, so I was confident my approach to the west wing would not be detected. I threw the camera switch again and now the camera in the hallway I was about to step out into was no longer being monitored by the security guards.

I quickly made my way to the west wing entrance. I lifted the cover on the fingerprint scanner and applied James' duplicate print to the pad. The pad beeped 3 times and I was unsure if it had accepted the print. After another second I heard the unmistakable sound of the solenoid locks on the metal door opening. I entered as quickly and quietly as I could.

I closed the door behind me and stood there with my back to the door trying to fathom what it was I was looking at. The room was rectangular (as depicted in the drawing), and while the walls all contained stations that might be consistent with some top secret experiment I could not take my eyes off what was definitely out of place in the middle of the room.

A VERY LARGE MANGO TREE.

The glass ceiling of the wing was at least 30 feet high and the size of the tree was such that the top branches just touched it. I approached the tree and noticed that there were numerous sensors hooked up to the soil surrounding the tree. I could see displays of PH, humidity, acidity and everything else to indicate that this room was designed to keep this tree healthy. As I wandered around the tree and gazed at the various stations on the walls I could find nothing in the room to indicate any other purpose other than the care and feeding of this mango tree. The tree was heavily laden with ripe fruit and while it appeared to be much healthier than any other fruit tree I had encountered I was trying to fathom how producing a better mango tree could be so valuable or secretive.

I thought my curiosity had peeked before coming into the wing but now I only have more questions than before. I saw nothing in this room that could be tied to Jack's death. No medical equipment or anything related to any of the special projects the DeLoreon Foundation had contributed so much money too. In my frustration for not finding any answers I instinctively reach up and picked a mango. I took one bite expecting there to be some revelation but it simply tasted like a mango. The most amazingly good tasting mango I have ever eaten, but still just a mango. I finished the mango as I walked around the room looking for clues. Feeling frustrated at seeing nothing at all related to the medical field, I picked a second mango in hopes that it might possess some enlightenment the first one didn't. No such luck.

I spent another five minutes frantically searching the room for clues. No locked safes, no locked containers, no secret filing cabinets, nothing other than an elaborate obsession with a mango tree. I glanced at my watch and noticed that it was now 1:45 p.m. As frustrated as I was that all my planning and scheming had gotten me no closer to solving Jack's death I figured it was time to do a quick departure here if I did not wish to face the consequences of my fraudulent entry into the DeLoreon estate. I snapped off as many pictures as I could with my miniaturized digital camera but was not optimistic these pictures would provide any valuable information later.

I opened the exit door, and to my surprise James Dewey was standing on the other side along with two security guards with drawn handguns. The guard on the left sprayed what I thought was mace in my face, but I felt no pain. Instead I started to feel light headed and stumbled backward. The room started to spin and I remember feeling a hard blow to the back of my head from the floor as I watched the skylight above me slowly fade to black.

Evidently, some time later I slowly started to gain consciousness and regain vision. I did not have a clue how much time had passed. I noticed I was in an office. I was facing a desk with a large painting on the wall behind it. I could make out it was a painted portrait, and the gold lettering below it simply stated "Governor of Puerto Rico". Sitting at the desk was obviously Joseph DeLoreon himself and I could now for myself see the scars that Jack had told me about last week. As my blurry vision slowly cleared I could make out the resemblance of Joseph in the painting. While it appeared to be Joseph, the portrait had none of the scars that were so visible on the face of Joseph sitting in front of me. I was unsure if this was a painting of Joseph prior to his disfigurement, or maybe the scars were intentionally left out during the painting process. But as my head cleared more I realized that my research of Joseph would most certainly have informed me if he was the Governor of Puerto Rico. So this must not be Joseph. Perhaps this was an ancestor of Joseph's that bore the same striking resemblance that Joseph's father did.

"I see you have awoken and we can begin discussing your presence on my island Mr. Gaites." Joseph said with a distinguished Hispanic ascent. "It was quite ingenious how you disabled our security systems. You can imagine our surprise when one of my security guards showed up on two separate video monitors simultaneously while performing his rounds."

I was still groggy and did not respond but only moved my head to gather more information about the room. At this point I realized I was restrained to the chair. As I glanced down at my restraints I was a little confused why I would be tied to a chair with what appeared to be small sheets, or maybe pillow cases instead of something a little more consistent with a well organized security force that controlled this island. Handcuffs I would have understood. It also finally occurred to me that Joseph addressed me by my real name and I wondered just how long I had been unconscious and just how long they had been investigating who I was. I brought no identification with me so whatever method Joseph used to identify me implied he had a sophisticated investigative team of his own.

"What is your purpose on my island Mr. Gaites?' Joseph said in a somber, quiet and yet firm voice.

I still ignored his question while again gazing around the room trying to gather by my surroundings what might be his intentions with me. I intentionally feigned less consciousness than what I was actually experiencing to try and buy more time to avoid acknowledging his questions. I know that Earl's access to the island ended up in his death but I felt some sense of security in the fact that Earl was performing a breaking and entering assault on the island that could justify deadly force. I on the other hand had simply gained access through fraud and deceit and I believed it would be hard for them to justify deadly force in my case considering my clothing and equipment would prove to the police that they had granted me access and that I was unarmed. Even though I was granted access through fraud, that would still not justify killing me.

"Mr. Gaites! If you ever plan to get out of that chair I would advise you to tell me your purpose on my island. I know the effects of my spray has worn off." This time Joseph spoke with a slight bit more volume and a little more irritation in his voice.

I responded.

"I'm looking into the death of a friend and trying to find out what part The DeLoreon Foundation may have played in that death." I figured if they knew my name they probably already knew that much. I would gauge my answers so as to appear cooperative until I could gather what their intentions were with me.

"We understand you have lost a friend Mr. Gaites. But what does that have to do with me and your presence on my island?" Joseph asked.

"I've already answered one of your questions. If you want me to answer your questions then you will answer some of mine." I responded.

"You are in no position to make demands Mr. Gaites. My island is a sovereign entity and I am free to do as I wish here. If you value your life and your freedom you will answer my questions." Joseph stood up as he stated this with yet another increase in volume.

It was obvious Joseph didn't know the exact purpose of my visit or how much I knew. Despite his upper hand in this situation he was frustrated at not knowing how much information I had gathered about him. His statement of my value of my life and freedom sent a slight shiver down my spine and I felt the necessity to see what his future plans were with me.

"Mr. DeLoreon. If you believe I have come here without anyone's knowledge you are sorely mistaken. Regardless of your power on this island I am still a United States citizen and my disappearance would be investigated. I have many friends in law enforcement that would get into your private business should I not return."

Joseph walked around his desk to me and appeared to be gauging a response. "I have no concern whatsoever who knows you are here Mr. Gaites. Answer my questions and you are free to go. Don't, and you will find yourself in a very uncomfortable situation until you do answer my questions. I am a very influential and powerful person and I can keep you indefinitely if needed to get the answers I need."

The fact that Joseph said he did not have a concern for who knew about my presence here eased my fear of Joseph erasing my life, but his last statement about an uncomfortable situation hinted at the fact that I might be in for some pain if I did not cooperate. I believed at this time he did not intend to kill me, but also did not plan on letting me go until I answered some questions. Time to open a dialogue.

"I will answer all your questions Mr. DeLoreon. But as I stated, you must answer some for me as well if you want my cooperation. You can get your information quick or I can drag this out for a very long time. If you have adequately done your research of me, then I am sure you know interrogation techniques will have very little success on me."

I could see Joseph was conducive to getting the information he desired quicker rather than drag this out. "Very well Mr. Gaites, what is it you desire to know?" he asked.

I knew I could not expect a direct answer if I simply asked if he had Jack killed. So I would ask questions to confirm various information I had that was as of yet unproven. I must also get across to him that I had incriminating information on him prior to my visit to the island such that my information against him would not be extinguished simply by erasing me and my visit to his island.

"You paid Jack Lambert a visit last week for a procedure on your facial scars and then went through a great effort to delete any record of your visit. You broke into his office and removed his file on you and your blood sample in an effort to erase any record of your visit. Why did you do this?" I wanted him to be in the dark as to what evidence I had concerning this, because while I could prove none of this in court, Joseph would have to wonder what information I had that led me to this conclusion. I hoped Joseph might consider the possibility that I possessed back-up files of his visit to Jack.

I could see a mixture of fear and anger in Joseph's eyes. "Yes Mr. Gaites. I removed those files. I live a very secret life. Jack demanded personal information I do not wish to become public. I conceded to give him the information in return for the procedure only because I planned on getting that information back later. It is very important that my personal life remain private. I could not risk the possibility of someone gaining access to Jack's files. My protection of my identity has nothing to do with your friends death though. Ok Mr. Gaites. I have answered one of your questions. What were you looking for on my island, and what information have you gained about my personal life inspiring you to risk your life coming here?"

"That would be two questions Mr. DeLoreon." I responded. Even though I knew there was a secret on this island that warranted an enormous amount of security, it seems that my knowledge of Joseph himself has struck a nerve. I could see that his fear of my being in possession of some of the information he might have given Jack was as important as whatever he was experimenting with in his west wing. I chose to avoid his first question because as of yet I still had no idea what I was looking for on his island. I felt as long as I was able to hide my ignorance of his island I might be able to gain some new information by exploiting his impatience with not knowing what I have already learned.

"I know you have gone through great lengths to hide your true identity Joseph." I threw out a first name there to give a hint I might know more about him than he believed I did. I continued to spout information in hopes of establishing that I had information stashed on him elsewhere.

"You have erased your birth records. You have taken care not to create any identification in terms of driver's licenses, voting registration, citizenship and everything else someone would use to track you down. You and your father John shared a great secret worth killing for." At this point I felt I needed to take a risk. I know that your Joseph is heavily into research for cosmetic surgery. I know I can find no record of his name prior to 1956, and I know that he appears to have changed very little in appearance since then.

"I also know that Joseph DeLoreon is not your real name, and cosmetic surgery is a part of your identity secret. You have poured a lot of money into this and other methods to protect your true identity."

Joseph's demeanor changed. His anger seemed to fade. I must have blown it and been wrong about my assumption, because it appeared he was no longer afraid of what I might know.

"So what is my real name then Mr. Gaites?" he asked.

I paused for quite some time, but realized that with the confident demeanor he now displayed that he knew I didn't possess that information. It now appeared that Joseph was less agitated and no longer considered me to be a threat. What could I have possibly said that changed his attitude so drastically.

"I don't know as of yet. That is the reason I came here. I know you killed my friend to cover up your visit to him." I replied. I saw no change in his smug demeanor at this point.

I calculated it was time to do a reversal on my original strategy. I now believed my best chance of getting released was to get Joseph to believe I possessed no real evidence against him. His sudden change in demeanor implied he did not consider me a threat, and my best chance for release would simply be to convince him I had nothing but suspicions.

"You are right Mr. Gaites. My name is not Joseph, it is Juan. Many years ago I had to make a choice. I could disappear from society, OR…" (he made a strong emphasis and paused after this word) "I could change my name. However, you appear to be wrong in many of your assumptions. I have not erased my birth records. I was born in Spain. My father shares no secret with me. My secret is mine alone. It appears your visit to my island was purely a hunch, and you possess no information that threatens me."

Joseph appeared to have the upper hand again and I was unsure as to why he was sharing this information. I couldn't understand what I had said that exposed my ignorance. His father built this island and the security wing that Joseph so adamantly guarded so how could he say he shared no secret with his father. My original sense of security had been based on convincing Joseph that I had sensitive information on him prior to my arrival on his island and I seemed to have blown that upper hand. So hopefully my new situation of not having anything harmful to him would work in my favor.

"You and I both know you are performing secret research here on your island. If I knew what it was I might be able to tie you to Jack's death. But if I have no information that threatens you then you have no need to keep me here further Mr. DeLoreon. Those who know I am here also know that I believe you to be responsible for Jack's death. My disappearance would only raise more suspicion than already exists. I suggest if you plan to press charges for my intrusion you do so now and turn me over to the Bahamas authorities."

"I do have a secret Mr. Gaites. But it does not involve research. Even though I do not believe you possess information that currently threatens me I believe you will continue to pry into that which does not concern you. You are a liability Mr. Gaites." Joseph pressed a button on his desk intercom and called for his security.

Panic was setting in at this point, and I needed to desperately convince Joseph it was in his best interest to let me go.

"Mr. DeLoreon! If you kill me, my friends will acquire information I possess that links you to Jack's death, as well as to the death of Earl Vedder in 1984. I have proof you paid Gloria Jansen $50,000 to fabricate her story to the police. My disappearance is not in your best interest."

The same two security guards I saw earlier entered the room and positioned themselves on either side of me.

Joseph turned to me and responded in a calm voice. "You have nothing Mr. Gaites. I am responsible for both the deaths of your friend and Earl Vedder, but my security force is very efficient at covering their tracks as they will be in your case also. You will not 'disappear' Mr. Gaites.

It appears you will acquire an unfortunate rare case of botulism from some of the fruit you have eaten back at your hotel on Bimini. It will also appear you made an attempt to contact help just before you died much as it appeared your friend Jack did. You will apparently be the victim of an unfortunate accident Mr. Gaites and it will be apparent that even though you intended on coming to my island, you never made it that far before your fatal accident."

It suddenly occurred to me why I was restrained in white linen instead of handcuffs. Joseph did not want to leave any marks. He never had any intention of releasing me.

"I have a wife waiting for me Juan. How can you do this and live with yourself?"

"I am not the horrible man you believe me to be Mr. Gaites. Many more people would die than you and your friend if my secret were to get out. I have an enormous responsibility on my shoulders and I have no problem living with the actions I am taking. The alternative would be to throw the world into chaos. My secret is too important to allow you to continue your prying."

As I frantically tried to think of a way out of this, Joseph signaled the guard on the left of me, and he sprayed me in the face with the same spray he hit me with in the west wing. As the room began to blur the guard on the right injected something into my right arm with a needle. I visualized my wife mourning my death as I slowly lost consciousness.

Chapter 10

Awakening

Again I experienced the sensation of slowly returning vision. Though the thought of an after-life was my first thought, I somehow figured an afterlife would not involve a ceiling fan. I stared at what I finally recognized as the ceiling fan above my bed in my Bimini hotel room for over a minute before I realized that I was unable to move. After another minute I was able to lift my head and I gazed down to see what was restraining my arms and legs and realized that there were no restraints at all. Moving my head back and forth I saw nothing out of the ordinary about my room with the exception of a turned over fruit basket spilled on the dresser and the desk chair overturned on the floor. After another 10 minutes of paralysis I was able to sit up in bed. I noticed my flip-open cell phone lay open on the floor. I also noticed banana peels and orange peels on the dresser now that I was sitting up and able to see the surface of the dresser. Something was not right. I was supposed to be dead. I remembered some of what I had heard about botulism from my emergency medical training in the police force and I knew that paralysis was one of the severe symptoms in cases leading to death. Suffocation due to paralysis of respiratory muscles was the fatal aspect of the disease. My symptoms seemed to be clearing up rapidly and from what I had learned about the illness, recovery from botulism normally would take weeks. Joseph seems to have botched up his assassination attempt.

If it were not for the fading effects of paralysis I would have jumped in the air as the room phone rang. My legs were still too stiff to stand but I was able to slide myself off the bed and pull the phone off the desk down to me by grabbing the cord. As I placed it to my ear I heard Marcy's voice.

"Jordy! Jordy! Are you okay?" she cried.

"Yes dear. I'm fine. Why do you ask?" I responded.

"You called me 30 minutes ago and all you did was breath hard and sound like you were choking. I tried calling you back but your cell phone isn't responding. I have been trying to get through to the hotel now for 30 minutes but all the lines have been busy. I just now got them to connect me to your room."

I thought a second and came up with a response. "I was choking on some fruit. I guess I knocked my cell phone off the desk while coughing and stepped on it. It must have auto-dialed you. I'm sorry dear. I didn't realize I had called you. I'm perfectly fine now though." I glanced at the clock and it was 4:30 p.m. I am not sure how long I was unconscious prior to my interrogation with Joseph, and I am not sure how long I was unconscious during my transport to my hotel room, but subtracting the amount of time I was conscious in Joseph's office I figure the two periods added up to about 2 hours. Assuming the two periods of unconsciousness were about equal in length and counting for the 30 minute boat ride I couldn't have been in my room much longer than the 30 minutes. This might mean Joseph's thugs could still be hanging around to confirm my demise. They were the ones who obviously called my wife to start the wheels rolling on the accidental death story. If they were in the lobby monitoring my wife's attempt to reach me then they might be watching the telephone switchboard and noticed that I answered the phone. Dead men don't answer phones. I needed to get moving fast.

"Honey, I've got to go now, I'll call you back real soon. I'm perfectly okay and am sorry for the scare with my choking, but I need to do something really important right now."

"But Jordy! Peter Kirby has been trying to get a hold of you all day." She exclaimed.

"Thanks Marcy. I'll contact him as soon as I get back. But I have to go now. Talk to you soon. Love you." I uttered as I hung up the phone.

I quickly grabbed a few things. Room key, cell phone. I then reached under the bed for my laptop but it was gone. I exited the room and headed to the elevator. It was on its way up from the lobby so I quickly dashed into the stairwell. After descending two floors, it occurred to me the stairwell exited in the main lobby and if Joseph's thugs were not on the elevator, but hanging out in the lobby it would not be in my best interest to waltz out and surprise them. I opened the 2nd floor stairwell door and glanced into the hallway. I noticed a maid knocking on a door as she loudly proclaimed "Maid Service!". I waited until the maid was satisfied the room was empty and she used her access card to open the door and then walked up. I flashed my room key (holding my finger over the room number), and informed her that I did not need maid service as yet. I then asked her if she would come back and collect my used towels later. She nodded and proceeded to the next room.

I remained glued to the peephole on the door for over 10 minutes without seeing any signs of Joseph's (Juan's) thugs. My concern at this point returned to my wife. I grabbed the room phone and dialed home.

"Hello?" Marcy answered.

"Marcy. It's me again. I need you to listen carefully. Joseph, or Juan, or whatever his name is has made an attempt to kill me and I am concerned about your safety. Please leave the house immediately and check yourself into a hotel. Do not tell anyone where you are going. Pay with cash and use a fake name. Turn off your cell phone now and keep it off until noon tomorrow. I will call you then and fill you in on everything. We can't delay talking about this now. You must leave the house immediately. Give me until tomorrow to sort this out and when I talk to you on the phone we can arrange a safe place to meet."

"Jordy. What is going on? What did you find out that caused him to try and kill you? Pete thinks he might have a lead on Mr. DeLoreon and wants you to call him."

"We don't have time to discuss this Marcy. I don't know if they know I'm still alive yet. I am worried that once they do they will try and get to me through you. Please leave right now and I will explain everything tomorrow. I am safe now so please don't worry about me. Just take care of yourself and wait for my phone call tomorrow at noon."

Certainly Mr. DeLoreon would be aware that I was not dead shortly if he wasn't already aware and I was concerned at what action he would take. Two things helped put me at ease a bit. First of all, he acknowledged that I don't really know anything damaging at this point. Second, he went out of his way to tell me he wasn't an evil person even though he was ordering my death. Maybe if he truly wasn't an evil person he wouldn't go after Marcy to get to me. But I needed some assurance. I needed to talk with him soon. But I didn't want to impede my attempts to escape Bimini Island prior to him being alerted to my recovery from his failed botulism cocktail. Using the stairs and a fire escape from the 2nd floor I was able to avoid the lobby and exit the hotel. I noticed the key to my boat was still in my shirt pocket, so I took a chance and went to the rental pier. To my pleasant surprise the boat I had rented was conveniently tied back up where I had untied it from this morning. I topped it off with gas and purchased an extra portable tank. It was about a 2 hour ride to Miami. I pulled away from the pier and got just out of site of the island and then killed the engine to make my phone call.

"DeLoreon Foundation. How may I direct your call?" The female voice answered.

"Please put Mr. DeLoreon on the line. This is Jordan Gaites and I need to talk to him at once."

"I'm sorry Mr. Gaites but Mr. DeLoreon doesn't take personal calls without an appointment. May I take a message?"

"He will take this call." I replied. "If you simply tell him who is calling he will speak with me immediately. If you chose not to disturb him I can assure you that Joseph will be extremely displeased with your decision."

I could tell by the silence and hesitation on her part that she was considering what impact her answer might have on her continued employment.

"One minute Sir and I will check." She replied.

After about a four minute wait James Dewey came online.

"Mr. Gaites?" He said with some obvious doubt in his voice.

"Nice talking with you again James. I need to talk with Juan right now. You refuse and I start calling the media."

"No need for that Mr. Gaites. I will transfer you now."

I heard the click of someone picking up a phone and then a short silence before Juan started speaking. I assume he was gathering his thoughts and trying to figure out how to acknowledge who he was speaking to.

"Mr. Gaites? May I assume you took your short time in my West Wing to eat one of my Mangos?"

This question was totally unexpected and threw me a curveball so I chose not to answer it. The mango must have possessed something to counteract the botulism virus he injected me with. So the mango tree had some medicinal aspect that might prove to be profitable after all. Still can't figure out a relationship between the healing properties of a mango and Jack's death.

"Juan, or whatever you want to be called. My priorities have shifted. I see there is no limit to what you will do to protect whatever secret it is you possess. My sole concern now is for the safety of me and my wife. You are still guessing that I do not possess any information now that you consider damaging. You were willing to kill me just to stop any further prying on my part. It's just this simple. If you or any of your thugs come anywhere near my wife I take everything I know, including your confession of murder, to every authority and media I can think of. Regardless of what proof I may or may not have, everyone loves a good scandal, and I can assure you I can put you, Jack's murder, and your magical mango tree in the lime light for a very long time. I have no problems with using unethical and illegal actions to make your life a living nightmare if you so much as get close enough to look at my wife. I can think of many fictional accusations to ensure every network takes heed and hounds you for a very long time. If you were to decide to take my wife hostage to force me to come to you, it will not work. I have no doubt you would kill both of us if I were to show up to obtain her release. My best course of action in that case would be to reveal everything I know and then bank on your statement that you are not an evil person. Once I have spilled my guts we would have no knowledge that everyone else doesn't also know and you would gain nothing by killing us. Your best chance to keep what I know a secret is to stay away from me and my wife. If you've done your homework on me properly you will know I have the ability to ensure whatever knowledge I possess goes public in the event of my death. Do I make myself clear Mr. DeLoreon?"

"Very clear Mr. Gaites. I see the logic in your threat. How would you propose we keep this strictly between me and you then? Do you plan on just forgetting my attempt to take your life?" Juan asked.

"You have stated that you are a very powerful and influential person and obviously very confident in your security force's methods of covering your tracks. Stay away from me and my wife for one week. If after one week I have not seen any attempts on your part to end my life again I will send to you any and all information I have acquired on you and your foundation and drop all attempts to investigate you. Kill me and regardless of the absence of proof, you and your foundation will be in the media spotlight for a very long time. On top of that I have some very close CIA friends who will take a personal interest in you. People love scandals and one involving three or more murders and industrial espionage can become a thorn in your side causing others to uncover information that I might not have been able to uncover. Leave me and my wife alone and I will forever become your silent partner that, as you put it, doesn't really know anything damaging about you anyways. However, if I see even one of your cronies near me or my wife, not only will I go public with everything I have now, but I will dedicate the rest of my life to revealing any and all secrets you protect. Do we have a deal Juan?"

"Everyone dies eventually Jordan. You expect me to leave you alone knowing that you are a permanent time bomb waiting to go off at any time for the remainder of your life?"

"In one week I will deliver to you everything I have learned. In one year I will destroy all information I have gathered on you. All this on the condition that you leave us alone to live out normal lives."

"We might be able to strike up a deal. I will expect you to deliver any and all information you have acquired on me in one week. But any attempts on your part to acquire more information on me will nullify our agreement. You understand this Mr. Gaites?" Juan asked.

I really didn't believe Juan (or whatever his real name was) had any intention of honoring his agreement but I believed this discussion might provide the stall tactic I needed to figure out my next step.

It was almost 7 p.m. before I saw Miami's skyline and I would have to rush to make my prearranged 9 p.m. return flight to Los Angeles. Knowing that my masquerade to infiltrate Juan's West Wing would be exposed by this time, I felt comfortable knowing that I had previously booked this flight under one of my old CIA alias' name. At least I no longer had any baggage to check for this flight. I grabbed a taxi near the pier I tied the boat up at and had him make a quick stop for me at a local electronic store to purchase a new laptop. I planned on making extensive use of the internet access now available on transcontinental flights for my return flight to Los Angeles.

I knew that my life as it existed now would never be the same unless I could either get rid of Juan or come up with some more information on him to release to the public. Once I found his secret and released it to the public I would no longer possess any information that everyone else didn't know. At that point he might still come after me out of revenge, but it was a risk I would have to take. If I was unable to uncover Juan's secret, then it was starting to look like killing Juan might be the only true solution to my problem. While I had killed in the past, I always took some comfort in the belief that I had only killed to preserve national security. Marcy's safety was much more important to me than national security at this point. I wasn't able to connect to the internet until we reached our cruising altitude but I had already formulated several new topics to search for when I finally was able to log in. My first search involved mangos and trying to connect the exotic fruit with any pharmaceutical or research companies. It seemed obvious that Juan believed my survival of his botched murder attempt was due to my eating his mangos. I could find nothing helpful about mangos on the internet to indicate what research Juan might be doing with the tree in his secret wing. My next search involved my half conscious conversation with Juan in his office. Juan's true identity might lead to answers to all of my questions, and there was an important clue hanging on the wall behind Juan's desk. All previous attempts to find leads associated with the DeLoreon name had been fruitless (no pun intended), and Juan himself had said that whatever secret he held required him to "either disappear OR change his name". The painting on his wall was almost certainly one of his ancestors and I know from the inscription on the painting that it was a former Governor of Puerto Rico. I had no idea how old the painting was, but considering the close resemblance to Juan I figured there might only be a generation or two separating Juan from his ancestor. Searching for Puerto Rico governors produced too many results to sift through on the flight, so I changed my search to only include photo archives. I got lucky and found a website that possessed photos or portraits of the majority of Puerto Rico's governors and I started right from the most recent governor at the top. As I was slowly scrolling through the photos I came across several with similar features to Juan, but none that matched the painting above Juan's desk. My optimism continued to fade as I scrolled further and further back in the chronological list of photos. My scrolling was faster than the loading of the portraits, so I commenced a new internet search while the last two pages of photos loaded. As I tabbed back to the portrait page, the last photo was downloading. It was a photo of the same painting that I saw over Juan's desk, and carried the notation below it:

Juan Ponce de Leon (1460-1521)
FIRST GOVENOR OF PUERTO RICO

I was stunned at the name as I slowly remembered my United States history class from high school where we all learned about the famous explorer who was credited for discovering Florida. But what made the hair stand up on the back of my head was my memory of what he was even more famous for. He was also considered a bit of a nutcase for wasting a good portion of his life looking for the mythical Fountain of Youth.

As I looked at the last name the conversation with Juan in his office became clearer. He said that he could disappear, OR (with a big emphasis on the word OR), change his name. I noticed the only difference between the name de Leon, and DeLoreon was the two letters "or". More goose bumps formed on my arms as I reconsidered the possibility of Juan being a descendent of Ponce de Leon and instead asked myself, "Could Ponce de Leon really have discovered the fountain of youth and still be alive today on North Cat Cay Island?" Could he be using the fountain to grow mangos with special healing properties?

The remainder of my flight home was spent brushing up on my history. History was unsure as to the actual date of his birth, but some history books placed his birth in 1460 while others report that evidence was uncovered showing that he was actually born in 1474. It appears that even though he was from an influential noble family his family genealogy was confusing both before and after he became Governor of Puerto Rico. What was meticulously recorded was his ventures in the Caribbean and his return to Spain to establish a new contract with King Ferdinand. Evidently, even though he was well established as a prosperous Governor of Puerto Rico Juan had something else in mind. As I continued to read my Wikipedia search about Juan's last visit to Spain I came across a rather unusual contract that Juan made with King Ferdinand:

"Ponce de León readily agreed to a new venture and in February 1512 a royal contract was dispatched outlining his rights and authorities to search for the Islands of Benimy. *The contract stipulated that Ponce de León held exclusive rights to the discovery of Benimy and neighboring islands for the next three years. He would be governor for life of any lands he discovered but he was expected to finance for himself all costs of exploration and settlement. In addition, the contract gave specific instructions for the distribution of gold, Native Americans, and other profits extracted from the new lands. Notably, there was no mention of a rejuvenating fountain."*

For the next nine years Juan continued his explorations of a very small area near Florida, and it was never recorded that he was searching for the Fountain of Youth. What is unusual about this contract compared to that of other aspiring Conquistadors at the time, is that Ponce de Leon was funding the exploration himself, and that gold and other profits would be returned to King Ferdinand. To the inquisitive history buff you would ask the question what motivated Juan to find the island of Bimini if it wasn't wealth. History records that on Juan's last island landing his expedition experienced a hostile attack from the natives and Juan was among the many to get hit by a poison arrow. Records show that he made it back to Cuba before his wounds became fatal. This was in the year 1521.

It wasn't until 54 years later that more information surfaced about Juan's ill-fated landing. Wikipedia contained information about a specific

Spaniard who had first hand information from the local Indians about Ponce de Leon's visit.

"*According to a popular legend, Ponce de León discovered Florida while searching for the* Fountain of Youth. *Though stories of vitality-restoring waters were known on both sides of the Atlantic long before Ponce de León, the story of his searching for them was not attached to him until after his death. In his Historia General y Natural de las Indias of 1535,* Gonzalo Fernández de Oviedo y Valdés *wrote that Ponce de León was looking for the waters of* Bimini *to cure his aging.*[34] *A similar account appears in* Francisco López de Gómara's *Historia General de las Indias of 1551.*[35] *Then in 1575,* Hernando de Escalante Fontaneda, *a shipwreck survivor who had lived with the Native Americans of Florida for 17 years, published his memoir in which he locates the waters in Florida, and says that Ponce de León was supposed to have looked for them there.*"

Evidently, even though his memoir was mostly about his life with the Indians, Hernando mentions the Indian's story about the "River Jordan" and it's healing and youth restoration properties and also mentions Ponce de Leon's expeditions to find the source of this water.

What if Juan Ponce de Leon actually found the Fountain of Youth and then returned to Cuba to fake his death? So was Juan's original contract with King Ferdinand to find the Islands of Benimy actually a quest to find the Fountain of Youth? I wondered if it was more than coincidence that Juan owned land on the Bimini Islands today. Could the Fountain of Youth be located on one of those Islands and Juan be using water from it to grow his experimental mango tree?

While I felt that I had more questions now than before about Juan's secrets I was starting to feel I had enough on Juan to create quite a stir in the media. I now believed that Juan broke into Jack's office because of his fear of what someone might find in his blood sample. While the vast majority of people would laugh this off as nothing more substantial than a UFO sighting, it would eliminate Juan's reason for trying to kill me. After all, I actually have no more proof of any of this than the typical alien abduction story. But it's not proof that Juan fears so much as suspicion. If I could generate a number of other curious people suspicious of Juan's identity, (regardless of how many of them would be nut cases), then eliminating me would no longer benefit Juan and in fact would lend credence to my wild story. Though wild stories usually require some evidence to inspire your typical conspiracy theory nuts, I believed the possibility of an actual Fountain of Youth would be enough to provide the push I needed to get this story into the media. That and the uncanny resemblance of Joseph DeLoreon to the painting of the real Ponce de Leon. His reclusive life-style, aversion to photographs and his land ownership on the Bimini Islands would just be icing on the cake to perpetuate interest in my story. I really didn't care who believed my story as long as I was no longer the solitary person privy to it.

For the last few minutes they allowed me to use my laptop before its decent I drafted my conspiracy theory in text complete with links to all the internet data I had uncovered. I included my theory about Juan's secret visit to Jack and now my newly formulated theory that Juan stole his blood sample and paperwork to prevent anyone from discovering any properties his blood might contain about his perpetual youth. Internet access had already been terminated as we began our decent as I was saving my document so I would connect again in the Los Angeles terminal to distribute my theory to various news agencies and law enforcement agencies.

Chapter 11

Home Again

Due to the time zone change it was still before midnight when I arrived back at LAX. There were numerous families at the departure gate waiting on relatives, but I didn't anticipate the black suited gentleman who approached me as I exited the boarding ramp.

"Mr. Gaites. We need to speak." He whispered.

I had informed no one about my return flight, so it was readily apparent this was another representative of my nemesis Juan Ponce de Leon. I stepped back from him and cautioned him:

"I must warn you, that this is a public place and anything happening to me here will only draw more interest into the criminal activities of your boss."

"I have no intention of doing you any bodily harm Mr. Gaites. I am only here to deliver a message."

"And what might that be pray tell?" I asked.

At this point he lifted his hand which I noticed had a cell phone in it. He opened the phone and pressed a couple of buttons, and then turned his phone to me to show me a photo. I vaguely recognized the photo of a motel on the beach I had stayed at once before.

"And what is that photo supposed to mean to me?"

"You might recognize it as, by our records, being a motel you stayed at on your honeymoon many years ago. It also happens to be the motel your wife checked into about three hours ago."

My face went flush. While I did now remember that this was in fact the motel we spent our honeymoon at, I intentionally didn't ask or tell my wife what lodging to acquire when I called her hours earlier. So even if they tapped my phone they couldn't have gotten this location from our conversation. Could this be a bluff? I spent a long time silently thinking without responding to the man. He became impatient and spoke again.

"There is very little information Mr. DeLoreon has not acquired about you since he first discovered you in his private west wing. Your credit card history shows you stayed in that motel long ago on your honeymoon, and that might explain why your wife chose to stay in that motel again tonight."

"Ok, I will concede I've stayed there before, but what proof do you have that my wife is staying there now and what is it you want from me?"

"Your cell phone and home phone have been tapped since we first identified you back on North Cat Cay Island Mr. Gaites. Mr. DeLoreon is quite aware of your conversation with your wife prior to your call to him. It was just a coincidence that one of our associates was preparing to enter your home to gather evidence when you made your phone call. He was instructed to follow your wife instead. If you look closely at this photo you will see your Suburban parked in the parking space on the far left."

I looked closely at the photo and even though the license plate was too blurred to read, I recognized the location of the Disneyland bumper sticker affixed to the rear bumper. The man continued with his threatening speech:

"We were also quite aware of your scheduled return flight to Los Angeles. And although we cannot nail down exactly whose laptop on the plane accessed certain files on the internet, the DeLoreon foundation has internet spiders to alert Mr. DeLoreon about certain subject matter searches, and it appears that the internet lines on your particular flight was flagged as having accessed our flagged subject matter. You have been a very bad boy Mr. Gaites, and Mr. DeLoreon has asked me to inform you that you are in breach of your agreement you just recently made with him. He has asked me to keep you company until he arrives in his private jet. He will be joining us shortly."

"And if I refuse?"

"Then I will be forced to call the gentleman sitting in the car outside your wife's motel room. Your wife is totally unaware of his presence and will remain so if you cooperate."

"And if I don't cooperate? I responded.

"This particular gentleman doesn't clean up messes, he makes them.

And I can guarantee that when he is done it will take more than a few hours to clean up your wife's room. Do you catch my drift Mr. Gaites?"

I was petrified. I knew what going with this man would mean for me, but I feared even more what would happen to Marcy if I didn't go with him. I only needed a few minutes to connect to the internet and share my file to protect myself and my wife, but I needed some way to warn her about the danger she was in. Evidently my hesitation was interpreted as a plot to escape the predicament I was in, and the gentleman spoke again.

"If you are thinking about warning your wife Mr. Gaites, need I remind you that while we know what room number your wife is in, you do not. If you remember correctly, you told her not to check in with her own name, and you also told her to turn off her cell phone. Being that we are almost a two hour drive from that motel I would venture to guess that you would be too late to save your wife if you decline to meet with Mr. DeLoreon. May I call Mr. DeLoreon and tell him we will both be waiting here to meet him when he arrives?"

I hesitated again, but could think of no way out of my present situation.

"Call your goon off. I will wait here with you. "

The man in the black suit then turned his back to me and made a quick phone call. I pondered a method to open my laptop and connect to the internet before Juan arrived. Juan's thug hung up and turned back to me and suggested we both get a cup of coffee in the airport diner while we waiting on Juan. I said that would be fine, but mentioned that I already had a lot of coffee on the flight, and needed to use the restroom to relieve myself.

"Feel free to relieve yourself Mr. Gaites, but, please hand over your computer and cell phone first. I will be waiting outside the door. You have three minutes. One second longer and I will be forced to call the gentleman waiting outside your wife's room."

I was off my game with all the surprises, and though I really didn't need to use the restroom I could come up with no miraculous plan to get out of this predicament in under three minutes. I did splash some cold water in my face while in the restroom to try and establish an alertness that might help but was still all out of ideas when I was escorted to the airport diner.

Not more than 30 minutes later Juan's thug escorted me to the arriving flights loading zone where a stretch limousine was waiting. I was motioned to get inside. Juan and James Dewey were both inside waiting on me and

Juan nodded to the black suited man through the window as he closed the door behind me. The thug walked to the other side of the limo and handed my laptop through the door window to James Dewey who then opened it and booted it up as we drove away from the loading area.

"I see you've been a very nosey person on your flight home Mr. Gaites." Juan sneered at me.

"Then you also know your secret is no longer a secret, don't you Juan Ponce de Leon?" I sneered back with his real name.

James' mouth dropped at this statement and it became apparent to me that while James might be Juan's personal assistant, it appears that he might not be privy to all of Juan's secrets.

"It just reinforces my original reasons for wanting to make you cease to exist Jordan." He retorted since we were now on a first name basis. "Keep in mind the reason I do not feel the need to keep a gun to your head at this point is because if I fail to make regular communication with my man stationed outside your wife's motel, he will enter your wife's room and dispatch her with extreme prejudice. And before you consider jumping me and forcing me to contact him, I must inform you that he will also request a password from me to ensure him I am not talking to him under duress. I hope you understand that I dislike guns greatly. Do you know exactly how many people are killed annually from accidental gun discharges Jordan? Please do not take the sign that I am not holding a gun on you as a sign of weakness."

"Making me go away will not make the information go away Juan. I've already compiled a full list of all my suspicions and what I know for fact."

Juan glanced at James, and James nodded to confirm that I had in fact created a file during my flight. I took another stab at Juan:

"So now that I've shared this information with everyone else, I have no more proof of your existence than the millions of others who will no doubt jump on board with this wild theory. You will gain nothing by killing me other than lending credence to the wild story I have distributed."

Again Juan looked at James, and again James nodded, but this time in a non affirmative manner. This time James spoke up.

"I see here you've done a pretty extensive internet search Mr. Gaites, but I also see that your so-called incriminating file was saved shortly before your flight landed, and there is no record of any internet access after that time and no record of any uploads or visits to internet based email services. While you are unaware of the vast information network control Mr. DeLoreon has acquired over the last few decades, we were slightly behind our game on this issue. Otherwise we would have been able to have terminated your flight's internet access before you acquired the information you did manage to acquire. I'm afraid your bluff won't work this time."

"If I have no evidence against you, then why the need to eliminate me and my wife?" I asked.

"Oh, but you do have evidence Mr. Gaites. **You** are the evidence. You ate one of my mangos, and for that I cannot let you live." Juan responded.

"Then you never planned on honoring our agreement from the start, did you Juan?"

"As neither did you Jordan."

As dire as my situation was, I still couldn't help but worry about Marcy's well-being.

"You have me Juan. Call your goon off my wife. You know I've shared nothing about what I've discovered with her."

"Unfortunately, I can't risk that. While your laptop leaves unmistakable evidence about your activities, I cannot read you like I can your laptop, so even though I tend to believe you have not shared anything with your wife, I cannot accept the risk. "

"But no one is going to believe we both had fatal accidents. I have friends in the police department that know about my suspicions. When we turn up dead you will be investigated."

"I'm okay with suspicion of murder at this point. After all, I've had to kill before to protect my secret. Suspicion of murder is not the earth-shattering story you planned to release with your little nosey file on your laptop. Your deaths will blow over when no evidence surfaces. But your Fountain of Youth conspiracy theory is not something that would blow over in a few days. I've checked your phone records and see you made personal calls to your police detective friend Peter Kirby and if need be I will have him eliminated also."

James looked up from my laptop and I could see he was intrigued by the fact that Juan mentioned my having a "Fountain of Youth conspiracy theory" without his having mentioned to Juan what it was that I had researched on the internet.

Juan nodded to James, and James pulled out a cell phone. I sensed this was the phone call to end Marcy's life.

"NO!" I yelled. "Do not kill my wife." James hesitated for a second looking at Juan, and I was frantically trying to come up with another stall tactic. Juan looked at James and nodded again to confirm the order to kill Marcy.

"Wait!" I blubbered. "I have evidence you don't know about. I've been saving it in case it came to this." Both Juan and James silently looked at me and I could see this bluff wasn't going to last long. I only had a few more seconds before James would continue with the call to end Marcy's life.

"Your blood sample. Jack always divides his blood samples in two and saves the 2nd sample as a back-up in case a patient has a serious side effect or rejection. You gathered up the back-up samples but forgot the sample he placed into his centrifuge the afternoon you showed up. Since no patients were seen subsequent to you, your blood sample was still in his centrifuge and I acquired that when I discovered your theft of his office. I have that sample in a safe place." I could see that I intrigued both Juan and James with this revelation. Juan motioned for James to put away his phone.

"Where is this blood sample Jordan?" He asked this question with the first bit of apprehension I had ever seen. I now had a slight crack in his power over me and I wasn't quite sure how to take advantage of this bluff.

"I've hidden it very well before coming to your Island. Keep in mind I knew that Earl Vedder was killed trying to infiltrate your island and I wanted a bit of insurance. I already knew at that point you had broken into Jack's office to steal all evidence of your visit. That blood sample was my proof you had visited him. An ace in the hole you might call it. I've attached a note to it saying that my best friend Jack was killed by Joseph DeLoreon trying to recover this sample of his blood along with the sparse information I had at the time. But it sounds to me that it's not the information I possessed at that time that scares you so much as the sample of your blood being analyzed. No doubt whoever eventually finds the sample will take it to the police."

"Where is that sample located?" Juan barked.

"I tell you that and you kill both me and Marcy. You need to come up with a method to ensure me that Marcy will be safe before I turn this sample over to you."

James opened the window to the front driver and whispered what I believed to be instructions for him to drive to my house. As short as the conversation was I wondered whether the driver had already been to my house at least once tonight. Evidently Juan and his thugs had also been very busy in the several hours since they failed to kill me in Bimini.

"How would you propose I do this Jordan. I doubt very seriously you will take my word for it that I will let your wife live if you turn over the blood to me."

"For starters, how about you convince me you have to kill either of us. If you feel so strongly that the Fountain of Youth must remain a secret then share with me why you are willing to murder me and Marcy over this."

"As I've said before, I don't kill because I enjoy it, I kill because I cannot risk the consequences of my secret getting out."

"And just what are those consequences Juan? How could the discovery of the legendary Fountain of Youth be a bad thing that you must kill others over?"

Extreme anger appeared on Juan's face. I could tell he was very uncomfortable discussing this in the presence of both James and his driver.

"**There is no Fountain of Youth!**" he yelled at me.

There was a long silence that followed. Juan was about to have me killed, and now he shares with me that I don't even know the reason. All along I thought his secret was the Fountain of Youth. I thought long and hard about my response, and then spoke as calmly as I could.

"Do you consider me to be a rational man Juan?"

"Yes." he responded

"And yet you want me to believe you are a rational man and not a cold-blooded killer. I have a blood sample that could blow the lid off of your secret, yet in your own words you will spare neither me nor my wife because of what we may know. Without any knowledge of why you are going to kill us you now ask me to hand over this blood sample. If you would like me to believe I am sacrificing our lives for a greater good, then share with me these dire consequences you talk of. After all, you have nothing to lose if you plan to end my life shortly. If you can convince me that revealing your secret is a bad thing, then maybe I will concede to give you the blood sample."

"How shall we start this 'rational dialogue' Mr. Gaites." Juan asked.

"Well, for starters, why did you not share your secret way back when you found it? Even if it's not the Fountain of Youth, you've discovered something that has prolonged your life indefinitely. Seems to me you would want to share this with the whole world as this would benefit mankind?"

"Benefit mankind?" Juan laughed as if I had made a joke. "Or be it's downfall? As I said before, there is no Fountain of Youth, but I will share my story with you Jordan, and perhaps then you will be inclined to believe I am not out for revenge on you and your wife, and that it is imperative that my secret not be revealed to the rest of the world."

Juan instructed James to handcuff me to the door and then get into the front seat beside the driver. Once James was in the front seat he instructed the driver to raise the sound-proof transparent partition separating the driver from the passengers. Juan then began his story:

CHAPTER 12

Juan's Story

"I AM, AS YOU MIGHT have surmised, Juan Ponce de Leon. I sailed with Christopher Columbus on his second voyage to America in 1493. I conquered Puerto Rico for Spain in 1509, became it's first governor, and became very rich in the process. It was then that I first heard the rumors of the island of Bimini and the fountain of youth. In 1513 I took a small fleet and searched for the island. Your history books credit me with discovering Florida, but Bimini was my great discovery. The natives were friendly and one of them had visited Puerto Rico and other islands in the Gulf over the years and learned Spanish. But they claimed ignorance when asked about the legendary fountain of youth. As we were leaving the island, we filled our water barrels with water from the mouth of the small fresh water rivers on the island we anchored next to. We joined up with one of my other ships that traveled south and discovered the islands you now know at North and South Cat Cay islands. Several of their crew has contracted Malaria, and were transferred over to my ship to be treated by the ship's doctor. He kept them isolated, but informed me their condition was grave, and they would probably not survive the trip back to Puerto Rico. However, after drinking water from our ship's water barrels they all had miraculous recoveries. When we returned to Puerto Rico, I safeguarded the remaining water and kept close tabs on my crew members from that fateful trip. I also had my personal physician perform routine checks on me to see if my water barrels in fact contained water from the Fountain of Youth. I needed to know if you only needed to drink once from the fountain or must continue to drink it daily. For several years, I alone drank one small cup of water from my stash in case the effect was not a permanent one. For the first few months none of my crew contracted any diseases or sickness. Eventually, the effect seemed to wear off of my crew. Over the course of the years many of them contracted diseases and illnesses, and some of them even died. I however, drinking my one cup a day, never came down with any illnesses, but my doctor insisted that he was still seeing some slight signs of aging. So in 1521, I gathered together another small fleet, and returned to Bimini to find the secret of this so-called Fountain of Youth. The natives on the island must have obviously known about the effects of the water, yet they kept it a secret from us. So I decided to try and keep my presence on their island a secret this time. The problem was that I would need to trace the small river to its source. The native's village was close to the mouth of the river so I would need to somehow locate the river upstream of the village without alerting them to my presence. I took 4 of my most trusted soldiers and one native of Puerto Rico who was capable of speaking the local language in case we encountered hostiles. We eventually found the river but as we started to track it we were spotted by a native hunting in the area. We were able to run him down and then questioned him. He tried to feign ignorance about the Fountain of Youth, but at sword-point, he became a little more talkative. He insisted there was no secret to eternal youth but only healing properties of the water. But when questioned as to the age of those in his village, it appears that the average life-expectancy of his village was well over 100 years. We took him with us as we continued upstream. I firmly believed that even if the river did not possess the secret to eternal youth, whatever lied at its source did. After another ¾ of a mile we came to a large depression in the terrain. About 4 different small tributaries contributed to a large pool of water. A large mango tree grew between two of them. I was now a little less confident of finding the source of the river's properties seeing as since the river was rapidly dividing into numerous smaller streams the further we tracked. We gave up tracing one of those streams when it became evident its source was just rainwater leeching from numerous vertical ravines looming ahead of us. We backtracked to the pool again and it was there we were attacked by a group of natives from the village who had spotted our anchored ship. Our translator said they were cursing us for violating a sacred forbidden place as they showered us with arrows. We dispatched them easily with our muskets, but Pedro, one of my soldiers was hit by an arrow in the shoulder. We removed the arrow and stopped the bleeding fairly quickly, but within minutes he was sweating profusely. Our captive native informed us the arrowheads were dipped in a very toxic poison and that outsiders rarely survived for more than an hour after being struck by one. I quickly ran to the pool and scooped some water in my hands and rushed back to Pedro. The native informed me it would be of no use unless the soldier had been drinking the water for some time prior to being struck by the arrow. He informed us that though the healing effects of the water would slow the effects of the poison it would not cure them. I chose to sit with Pedro for the next hour since I knew his family back on Puerto Rico. I listened to his last wishes to share with his family upon my return to Puerto Rico. As the poison progressed he expressed an unquenchable hunger and thirst. I gave him more water and sent another soldier to the mango tree to fetch him a few mangos. Over the next hour his symptoms did not seem to get any worse though he still possessed a great fever. But then over the next hour his symptoms started to clear up. The other 3 soldiers were devout Catholics and had been praying for his soul the previous hour, and accredited his recovery to their prayer and their faith in God. I however grew curious and wandered over to the Mango tree, and noticed that as the fruit grew ripe and dropped from the trees many of the mangos fell into the two streams that fed the pool of water. I immediately suspected that the mango tree and not the water was the source of the healing properties. Evidently, even the natives to the island were unaware of this and never ventured this far from their village to partake of the tree's fruits. Taking care the others did not see, I stuffed a mango in each pocket. We retreated to our ship, but as we were rowing to my ship we were attacked again by the natives. Each of us took at least one arrow. I took one to the leg and one to the shoulder. Pedro, the crew member who was already wounded, took one to the head and was immediately killed. The four of us were hauled up into the ship's dispensary and we immediately set sail for Havana. The other three soldiers did not survive long enough to reach Havana, but I ate my two mangos while we were rowing from Bimini to my ship. I did exhibit the same fever as Pedro did but I felt confident the mangos would protect me from the effects of the poison as they did Pedro. My reasoning was that Pedro did not eat his one mango until he had severe symptoms, while I ate two of them immediately after contracting the poison. I had a close confidant in Havana who saw our ship approaching and met us as we docked. He assisted in transporting me to Havana's dispensary. My symptoms were cleared up before we ever even sailed into Havana but while lying in my cot on the ship I realized the significance of my find. I was worried others might steal my discovery if I revealed it. I developed my plan even as my fever was still with me before reaching Havana. My confidant arranged to have all my wealth transferred to Havana, and once it was there we arranged for the news of my death to be released to the public. I went underground and took a new name. Slowly over the next few months I acquired a band of mercenaries to accompany me back to Bimini. This time we approached from the opposite side of the island and cleared a path large enough to dig up and transport the mango tree to my fleet of ships. While I have no doubt the mercenaries believed me to be some eccentric fool with a passion for mangos, they were willing to tolerate my eccentricity for the amount of gold I paid them. I acquired the uninhabited island of North Cat Cay to plant my tree, and then slowly built my estate around it. I acquired some of the most discreet staff I could, including a doctor to examine me over the next few decades But none of them had any idea who I was or what my secret was. It became immediately apparent that drinking the water downstream of where the mango tree was planted as the natives had done only provided them with a very small fraction of the properties of the fruit. Enough to provide healing properties and double life-expectancy but not much more. I had a grandiose plan to find a way to peddle my mangos to the rest of the world. My intent was never to keep this gift to mankind a secret, but only to profit from it. But first I must study it. I must know whether off-spring from it's seeds would also possess it's elixir of youth. If others were able to grow trees from the seeds, it would severely affect my profit. As the years went by I grew some 2nd and 3rd generation trees, and their fruit also proved to possess the same youth halting effect as the original tree. If I were to effectively market the fruit, I must not allow anyone to acquire the seeds to grow their own trees. Performing experiments on rats I was able to determine that eating just one mango was enough to invoke an almost permanent age-halting effect. But as I studied the effects of the fruit reality slowly started to set in. First of all, the fruit did not produce immortality as evident by Pedro's death. It only stopped the aging process and made the body immune to virtually all known diseases. Make no mistakes Mr. Gaites, by you eating a mango from my tree, you have ensured you will never age another day the rest of your life. But there are many ways to die other than old-age. I was 61 years old when I ate the mangos, and though I will never age, I also will never get any younger. I experimented with many different animals, and discovered the effect was always the same. It halted the aging process at whatever age the animal was when it partook of the mango. I began to examine my plan for marketing my product. If I could not supply the whole world with the fruit at once, who would I provide it to first? What would happen when one country found out another country had possession of a fruit that gave 'eternal life'? I foresaw horrible wars taking place to be the owner of this fruit. At what age would one partake of this fruit? If we gave it to our children, they would never age. They would grow smarter, and develop the mentality of an adult, but would never outgrow the adolescent hormonal experience. What about the aged people? They are the ones who possess the world's wealth and would want the fruit the most. From my experiments with animals, I learned that while the fruit halted aging, it would not correct crippling injuries. It would not grow back lost limbs. While cuts and injuries would heal quickly, the long lasting scars or debilitation from injuries would remain. The loss of endurance and strength that comes with age would also not be cured. Who would financially support the ever growing number of invalids incapable of performing an occupation? Not to mention the impact on our present expectations of working hard for about 30-40 years, and then enjoying the fruits of our work, no pun intended, for the rest of our lives. How long would someone who is capable of work be expected to work? After all, our society's concept of retiring around the age of 65 is based on only needing money to survive for another 20-30 years after retirement. No company will offer a retirement plan expecting to pay retirees for a potentially unlimited amount of time. Would we then come up with a plan to euthanize anyone incapable of producing an income so the rest of us don't have to endlessly work for centuries to support them? And even if you are healthy and capable of work, if you live long enough you will eventually have a disabling injury that the mango cannot correct. Death would be limited to those experiencing traumatic accidents. If someone would become crippled and confined to a nursing home, what are the chances they would encounter a traumatic accident at that time? Nursing homes would slowly fill up with people who have debilitating injuries and yet will most likely live forever. If our world could survive the chaotic wars that would inevitably break out to claim possession of this miraculous Fountain of Youth, our society would then break down based on the loss our current naturally evolving family process. The current concept of slowly experiencing the joys and woes of growing up and growing old would cease to exist. How many times have you heard the expression, 'Well, enjoy yourself, you're only 40 once?' What if that weren't true? What if you were 40 forever? We are already experiencing overpopulation even with our world's present high mortality rate. With 7 billion people in our world, it is safe to say that 99.9% of them will be dead 100 years from now. What if suddenly we decided that the reverse would be true? What would happen if we suddenly reduced that mortality rate to near zero? My concern for overpopulation was solved very quickly with my next discovery. I have not even gotten to the worse side effect of all.

Sterility. A mango treated male cannot produce the seed needed for insemination. And even if you could obtain a growing male seed, a mango treated woman would pass her blood into her fetus which would then not develop in her womb. Would you want to present the world with the gift of eternal life at the cost of never producing any off-spring? But of course the rich who partake of the fruit could always adopt, right? That would imply the world would have to separate into a caste system to survive. There would be those who lived forever and those who lived a relatively short period of time for the purpose of procreation. I came to the conclusion long ago that I could never share my secret with the world. I am still experimenting with a possible fix to the sterility issue among other issues but I don't see any breakthroughs in sight. When I first discovered the tree I lived in solitude only rarely venturing out in public for over 50 years. I was slowly dying emotionally so I eventually surfaced in public again claiming to be my own son. I again took the office of Governor of Puerto Rico and I even took a wife. I did not share my secret even with her, in the hopes that I could overcome the sterility issue and produce a child with her. Though she did grow suspicious at my lack of aging over the years it was both incredibly painful, and a blessing in disguise when she died prior to discovering my secret. I stayed in the public eye for a few more years and then again dropped back into solitude. In the early 1900's I returned to Bimini with some scientists and we were able to determine that the youthful effect on the natives had dissipated since I removed the tree. We were also able to determine that sometime in the distant past a meteor had struck the island causing the depression that contained the pool of water and the magical mango tree. I have no doubt that the secret of the mango tree did not originate on our world but instead came as a by-product from that meteor strike. Also in the early 1900's, a hurricane struck my island and one of my large windows on my estate imploded on me causing the severe lacerations you see on my face and hands. The wounds healed quickly but the scars remain. This inspired me to invest vast amounts of money into cosmetic surgery. I've also lost a finger in the mid 1800s and I contribute large amounts of money toward the research of prosthetic limbs. I have to face the fact that if I am not killed in some unfortunate accident, I will eventually be maimed with the loss of an arm or leg. As I mentioned Mr. Gaites, I am not immortal. I just don't age. Are you starting to fathom the magnitude of the secret I possess? What would we do with the ever-growing amount of ageless sterile invalids that would most assuredly become a by-product of introducing this fruit to the world? If I were to share this with the world, man-kind would cease to exist as we know it today."

Juan stopped talking and we were both silent for over a minute while I tried to grasp the enormous burden he has kept secret all these years. I finally responded.

"Yes Juan. I believe I understand the enormous weight you are carrying with this secret and I agree the world is not ready for this secret. How is it that you trust your employees with your secret but you are not willing to trust me?"

"James here is the only other person in this world that has partial knowledge of my secret. But until you started prying he only knew that I was experimenting with a mango tree that has miraculous healing properties. He is also aware that it produces sterility, and is therefore content for me to keep my secret from the rest of the world until I am able to overcome this obstacle. I screened James thoroughly for the position he holds. James had almost all of the key attributes I was looking for in the perfect profile for someone who would take a secret to the grave with them. James' sister was dying of cancer. I made a pact with James that I would cure his sister's cancer and set his family up with enough money to ensure they and their offspring would never have to work again if he were to come work with me and ask no questions about my research. I have given James' sister her life back and most likely extended it by 10-20 years beyond her normal life expectancy. But James also knows that I can just as easily remove it if I am crossed. I do not doubt his loyalty. James worked for me for twelve years before I was confident enough to reveal the mango tree to him. But he only knows of it's healing properties, and while I believe he suspects it also affects my aging, I have never shared with him my story of the Fountain of Youth. He has been quite happy with our arrangement and does not judge me for not giving him my curse of prolonged life. You have jeopardized this relationship I have with James. So do not even consider pleading with me to trust my secret with you Mr. Gaites? How long would it be before you share this with another, and then another? How long before your wife becomes suspicious that you never age or get sick? No Mr. Gaites, unfortunately I cannot risk the fate of the world based on my compassion for the life of one person. As I told you, I am not a monster. I am simply forced to choose between the lesser evil. Killing a single individual or risking the destruction of our world's society. I might still be inclined to leave your wife alone if you can turn over your blood sample to me. Knowing the risk you were taking with your coming to my island I am fairly confident you did not share this information with your wife. If you had, she probably would not have allowed you to come. If you give me the blood sample I will assure you that your death will be painless and that your wife will be financially secure the rest of her life."

I still doubted Juan's sincerity of sparing Marcy's life but I must continue my bluff in hopes of coming up with some way to get the drop on Juan.

"The blood sample is in my fire-proof safe. It's a hidden wall-safe with a retinal scanner I acquired from my days in the CIA." I figured if I simply gave him a location he could access himself, he would have no reason to keep me alive.

"Very well Mr. Gaites. I appreciate your cooperation and promise you that your wife will be well taken care of for the remainder of her life. I also assure you that if I am able to overcome the sterility issue and foresee a solution to the other problems this fruit will thrust upon the world that I will see to it your wife gets the opportunity to partake of the fruit if she so wishes."

The visit to my house would buy me some time to try and think of a way out of this mess. Escape was not in my plan since I couldn't risk Juan triggering his assassin outside Marcy's motel. Juan pulled out a device from his breast pocket that looked like a cell-phone yet only had 4 or 5 buttons on it. He pressed a button on it and returned it to his breast pocket. He noticed my curiosity and explained:

"Keeping your wife safe for a bit longer. She's still my insurance policy to ensure your cooperation."

Evidently keeping my wife safe required a periodic signal from Juan using this device.

Chapter 13

No Way Out

As we drove to my house I tried to figure out a way to access my spare gun taped to the bottom of my desk drawer. I hadn't thought this out all the way when I mentioned my safe was in the wall. When we arrived at my house the driver continued around the corner and parked in the back alley. It was close to 1 a.m. when we arrived, and even though I doubt anyone was awake to see who was parking in my driveway I suspected that Juan planned to leave me dead in my own house and would prefer not to have some neighbor tell the police there was a limousine in the driveway. James exited the car first and as he leaned towards the door to open it for Juan I saw a gun concealed in his jacket. Evidently, even though Juan had mentioned his aversion to guns, James was packing one. I believed my presence overrode Juan's fear of guns. Juan's driver also exited the vehicle and I felt fairly sure that he would also be in possession of a gun. The driver stayed ahead of me while we approached the back of my house while Juan and James stayed behind me. It was obvious that Juan's employees had preset functions for situations such as this and I concluded that the driver most likely had other duties besides driving. Considering James was Juan's personal assistant with business and financial duties, I decided that the driver was probably the first person I should deal with if I were able to obtain my gun. The driver opened the back door and walked in first. Since I doubt that Marcy left the house unlocked it was apparent that my house had already been searched.

"Be quick about this Jordan. I do not wish to disturb your neighbors. Please get me my blood sample."

"The retinal scanner has to be activated from my computer." I stated as an excuse to approach my desk.

James motioned to the driver who escorted me to my computer desk and stood to my left as I sat down. James came to the other side of the desk and stood to my right and watched my computer screen. Grabbing my gun while these two were scrutinizing my every move was going to be difficult. I raised my knee to locate the guns exact position under my drawer and my heart sank. Juan intentionally allowed me to sit at my desk to further reinforce the futility of my situation.

"If you're looking for your gun, it was removed earlier tonight." Juan exclaimed. "You don't really have a 2nd blood sample do you Jordan?"

I just sat there motionless. I was out of options. I could see that James had his hand inside his coat near the place I saw his gun while leaving the car. Even Juan himself had his hand in his coat pocket and I was confident he was ready to communicate with his assassin using the device I saw earlier. Even if I were to miraculously disarm all three men I would most likely still lose Marcy in the process.

"You're not going to get away with this Juan. There will be evidence pointing to you."

"You're wrong Jordon. Our first visit to your house tonight wasn't just to look for evidence. We've manufactured a plethora of evidence to prove you and your wife were targeted by a gambling ring you were hired to investigate. Even your trip to the Bahamas fits within our scenario. It will be difficult to link either of your deaths to us."

"You said you would spare Marcy!" I pleaded.

"That was before this final futile attempt to deceive me Mr Gaites."

Juan pulled his hand out first. But instead of the device he held earlier he held a Motorola which he began to speak into.

"Julio, eliminate her with extreme prejudice." he shouted angrily into the device and I saw no remorse with this command.

"No I shouted. Marcy forgive me." I shouted as I dove over my desk towards Juan. My rage overrode my initial plan to attack the guard first, but I didn't care if I was shot in the back as long as I could get my hands on Juan's throat before I died.

Then all hell broke loose. Juan escaped my lunge and moved to my left. I was temporarily shielded from James and the driver by my desk. As I got to my feet and turned towards Juan I could see the driver had his gun drawn and pointed at me. I could feel the wind of his first shot on the tip of my nose and then as he started to squeeze off his second shot I heard the crash of my living room window and saw him fall to the floor. I turned towards the window and saw Pete Kirby in the lower left corner of the window with his gun drawn. Both Juan and James spun towards Pete and as James fired his gun at Pete Juan pulled out a gun. I hurled myself towards the fallen driver to grab the gun still held in his clutches. Out of the corner of my left eye I could see James violently spun counterclockwise by a shot to his left shoulder. As I pulled the gun from the dead driver's hand. I turned to my right to see Juan starting to fire at Pete. I got off two shots into Juan's chest and the third caught him in the neck as he was falling. Shortly after the gunfire began I could hear the crash of the front door and two of Pete's fellow officers entered the room just as the gunfire ended.

The whole ordeal was over in just under 10 seconds though it seemed much longer. The smell of gunpowder and the haze of gun smoke filled the room. I could see that Pete was yelling something to me through the window but my ears were ringing and I was unable to hear him. Two more officers burst in from the rear door. I plopped down in my desk chair and gazed at the 3 men on the floor. Juan's driver was obviously dead from his wounds. James appeared only wounded in the shoulder, but his gun had fallen several feet away from where he laid. My shots had struck Juan in his chest yet I saw no blood on his white shirt. I glanced at James and he was watching me and knew my question in advance.

"Juan always wears a Kevlar vest whenever he leaves the island." James stated matter of factly. My hearing was slowly returning but it was more lip-reading than hearing that informed me what he had said..

I looked back at Juan and noticed the glancing blow to his neck appeared to have done more damage than I thought as he was severely bleeding from that wound. Though he seemed lifeless I could tell he was fully aware of what was happening around him and he was looking right into my eyes. His gun had also fallen out of his left hand and he was in no shape to crawl to it. I could see pain in his eyes as he slowly moved his right hand to his coat pocket. I kept my gun pointed at him in case he had another concealed weapon. Instead he pulled out the same device he used in the car and pressed three buttons on it and then looked back at me. About 5 seconds later the device fell out of his hand and he appeared to have lost consciousness from the loss of blood. The two officers quickly rounded up the loose guns while keeping their guns pointed at my assailants. Pete was now leaning through the broken living room picture window.

"Jordy, are you alright?" Pete asked.

"Yes Pete. Quickly get someone to the Sunset Motel in Long Beach I shouted." Pointing at Juan "he just signaled one of his thugs to kill Marcy and I think we might be too late to save her."

"No we're not Jordy, she's out in th……." but before he could finish his sentence Marcy came rushing in behind the officers who entered the front door and ran to me. As we embraced, Pete rounded the corner of the house and entered the same door Marcy entered.

"Pete how….?" I didn't know what question to ask first. How he had known where Marcy was at, or how he had known to come to my house.

"I've been trying to get a hold of you for two days now Jordy. I did some more investigating based upon a few things I discovered. I remembered you telling me that Jack wouldn't buy cheap wine so I checked with the coroner. A preliminary autopsy suggested that Jack had no alcohol in either his bloodstream or stomach which didn't jive with the opened bottle. I was also thinking about the locked door. I looked at the lobby video again, and sat down with the hotel clerk on duty that night. Though he could not be 100% sure he was fairly confident that one couple that showed up on the video 30 minutes before Jack's death had checked into a room directly above Jack's room three hours earlier. They paid with cash in advance and their key was left in their room when they departed so that we don't have a check-out time. I checked out their room and found a slight mark on his railing that could indicate someone used a rope to lower themselves onto Jack's balcony from the balcony above. I did some further research into your suspicions and while I still did not have any conclusive evidence linking the DeLoreon Foundation to Jack's death I found some unsettling coincidences that I needed to talk with you about. Then Marcy called me to ask for help. She told me about your phone call and I immediately sent out two officers to stake out her motel room. They called me when they arrived to inform me there was a suspicious person sitting in a car near her room. We picked him up almost three hours ago and identified him as an employee of the DeLoreon Foundation. He cracked under the threat of being charged as an accessory to your murder if he didn't help prevent it. He admitted to following Marcy to the motel and also to being in contact with others who broke into your home earlier this evening. I dispatched an officer to stake-out your house in case they returned and he called me when you arrived in the limousine. I'm sorry it took us so long to arrive with back-up, but it appears we got here in the nick of time.

I turned to Marcy. "But they had your cell phone tapped and would have known you called Pete."

"You told me to turn off my cell phone and call no one Jordy, so I did that. But then I grabbed one of your untraceable Go-Phones in your desk and called Pete to ask for help and tell him where I was going.

What in the world have you gotten yourself into Jordy?" Pete asked.

"It's a long story Pete. Can I just have a few minutes to talk with Marcy and ensure she's okay before we go over this?"

"She's fine Jordy. I told her to come down to the precinct and wait for me to figure this out but when I got the call from the officer staking out your house she insisted on coming along."

"Let's get this scene stable!" Pete barked to the other officers. "Let me call this in Jordy while you and Marcy calm your nerves." Pete got on his radio and started informing the precinct of our situation and requesting medical assistance.

I turned my attention to Juan again. While the pool of blood beneath his head was still spreading, the flow of blood from his neck was no longer pumping. It appeared he died while Pete and I were discussing the situation. I turned towards James, and saw that he was painfully attempting to get into a sitting position while one of the officers was cuffing his hands behind his back.

"So, James. It appears you no longer have an employer and also have a lot of explaining to do. How are you going to explain what's going on back on Juan's island?" I asked.

"I might not know all the answers to the questions that will be asked, but explaining what exists back on Cat Cay won't be necessary Mr. Gaites. What you saw Juan do with that device was send a signal to the island. In a situation such as this either Juan or myself were supposed to signal the island. The whole west wing is most assuredly up in flames as we speak. I have come to respect Juan over the years and I have no doubt that his destruction of the west wing was in the world's best interest. While I am not happy for taking the fall for what Juan has done, at least in my heart, I believe Juan when he says that what we were doing was necessary for the better good of the world. I will have to face up to the responsibility of what we've done but I still have the peace of mind knowing that my family will be well taken care of in my absence. I anticipated this day would eventually come. But wouldn't you do almost anything to save a loved one Mr. Gaites? My sister is alive today because of Juan."

The realization of what just happened and what James was sharing with me now was setting in. Not only was I free to return to my wife without fear of Juan or his assassins, but it appears that I alone possessed the full secret that Juan was keeping from the world. At this point, with the mango tree destroyed, I felt confident that if I were to share the truth about what existed in that west wing, or who Juan really was, I would be locked up in a funny farm. This all sounded like science fiction to me now that both Juan Ponce de Leon and his Fountain of Youth mango tree no longer existed.

I spent 3 hours down at the precinct giving my statement. I shared everything I knew about the DeLoreon Foundation's involvement in Jack's murder with the exception that I only speculated on possible motives. I simply implied that with all my investigation I never really discovered the specific reason for Jack's murder. It appears that the police were considering the murder to be based on attempts on Juan's part to steal technological information from Jack. The sun was beginning to rise as we left the police station and Marcy and I were both famished. We stopped for a quick breakfast at Denny's where I proceeded to tell Marcy the whole truth about Juan and his mango tree. While there was obvious disbelief on her part concerning the actual identity of Juan early in the story, I could see that she knew me enough to realize that I was not insane. In the end she simply conceded to say that she believed that Juan told me what he did and that I did not imagine any of the previous day's events. But I could tell she doubted the validity of what Juan had told me. She responded by saying that the world will never know the truth and we would be wise to not share anything as unbelievable as the story I just shared with her.

Due to the shambles our home was in, Marcy and I checked into a posh downtown hotel to try and recover from our ordeal. I hadn't slept in well over 24 hours and desperately needed a shower and change of clothes. I chose the honeymoon suite at the Waldorf for our recovery and we were able to check in at 8 a.m. and only have to pay half price for the previous night. Marcy objected to the cost at first but I ironically reminded her how short our lifespan was and how close we had both come to death today. I could see the twinkle in Marcy's eye as she was contemplating the validity of Juan telling me I would never grow old. Jack's death had inspired me to decide that we needed to enjoy our lives while we could. She laughed at this. We both got out of our dirty clothes and Marcy had a posh terrycloth Waldorf robe waiting for me when I got out of the shower.

"Are you aware you have blood stains on your pants from your gun battle that trashed our home Jordy? I've called room service and they will be up shortly to take our clothes out to the cleaners." Marcy said.

"Well, you know the life of a Private Eye. I'm only upset that I cannot share this case with Jack. This was exactly the type of suspenseful story I had hoped to share with him during his dinner with us at our house. I wanted so badly to prove to him my life was not mediocre compared to his lucrative career."

"Our life will never be mediocre." Marcy said as she removed my wallet from my pants. Then Marcy looked at me inquisitively and asked:

"Jordy. What would you like me to do with these two mango seeds you have in your pants pocket?